CALLIOPE VALE

Chestnuts

CHESTNUTS

Cover Illustration and Typography by
Lorissa Padilla
https: // www. lorissapadilla.com/design

ISBN 979-8-9890410-8-4 *(print edition)*

ISBN 979-8-9890410-9-1 *(ebook)*

1 2 3 4 5 6 7 8 9 10

www.calliopevale.com

For all who thanklessly
make holiday magic happen.

It's time someone (or two)
took care of you.

Content Warning

This is a very spicy why choose MMF novella which means that in the end, our protagonist ends up with two Christmas elves and get her happily ever after.

All scenes are consensual. Use of safe words is discussed but never needed.

However, there may be some aspects of this book that readers might need to approach with caution including:

Alcohol consumption
Light BDSM elements
Threesome with two men
Magical transformations without consent
(fixed quickly)

Author's Note:

As this is a novella, the magic system may be soft but the dicks are rock hard.

This is all in good fun. So with that in mind:

If you're here for a rich plot full of political intrigue and deep world building, this book wont be fun.

If you're here for a good time, a relatable protagonist, and Christmas magic, then you'll have a blast.

If you are my family or friend IRL and somehow found this book-- thanks for your support! Also, you absolutely must put this down immediately.

I'm not joking.
Put it down.
Walk away.
pls.

I love you all.

CHAPTER 1

Fucking Greg. Not like That

"Remember how mom used to say she'd spent *all day* on Christmas dinner? And she was like 'you better be grateful because I just spent all day in the kitchen'?"

"I was never grateful for those mushy green beans." My sister's voice laments through the phone speaker.

I flop onto the couch and sigh, though it comes out as more of a groan. I hold the phone closer. "Well, she never spent more than an hour on dinner, that's the point," I say as I throw an arm over my eyes, shutting out the depressing scene before me. "I *literally* spent all day on this party though. And only one person showed up. Greg."

"Remind me," my sister says dryly.

She's bored. As I spill my sorrow. *Rude.*

"Greg!" My voice comes out shriller than I would like. I sound hysterical.

I've told her about Greg *a lot* throughout my last few months working at the new gig. But he must be blander than I thought because she forgets him every time. "The guy from the office. The one I went out with once," I say, trying to jog her memory.

"Oh," she says. "Right, the one who took you to Taco Bell. I thought that was kind of nice. Thoughtful, you know?"

"On a first date, Krista?" I pull my arm free from my face and blink up at the twinkling colorful lights I had meticulously hung from the ceiling. I nearly died on that rolling office chair setting them up and no one even showed up.

Except Greg.

Who took me to Taco Bell on a first date because it has 'lots of vegetarian options'. *I guess that was kind of thoughtful.*

I sigh again. Perhaps my mom was right and I am just an ungrateful person.

Still, my sister concedes. "Alright, yeah, not great for a first date." She pauses, as if considering something. "You really spent all day setting the party up?"

All around me, the fairy lights I hug all across the studio apartment twinkle, blinking gently. There are *three* different Christmas trees, decorated in plastic gold and the little ornaments from my youth. There's fake wrapped presents beneath them to make it look like the holiday was *abundant.*

I hate that word. Such a new age buzz term.

Abundant.

Act like you are and it shall be.

I put it on my vision board, and all I got was this. An empty studio on a frigid night.

What a load of bullshit.

Hand-cut snowflakes hang on invisible strings descending from the ceiling, all unique. I want to rip them down, but I'm afraid I've had one too many glasses of wine to risk getting back up on that wheelie chair.

I try to pull my sister back on my team. "I made a bunch of different themed cocktails. A pie. And, like, so much charcuterie."

"You did not *make* the pie," my sister says.

She's right. I can't bake. Or cook really.

"I bought it and set it up and made it look cute," I argue.

She lets out a long breath. "Alright, little orphan Annie." She uses the silly nickname from our childhood, clearly trying to cheer me up. All that happens is a few tears sting the corners of my eyes. The name reminds me of all the times she spent the holidays chasing me around, telling me that the Ghost of Christmas Past was coming for me and that Santa was watching me while I slept.

Even so, I'd kill for her to be here now, teasing me again like she used to. Even if I were still afraid of that dumb movie with the creepy ghost. And terrified of some guy watching me all night.

"This does suck," she says. "I'm sorry no one came. I wish I were closer. I'd come help you clean up."

I notice she says 'help clean up' not, 'I'd come to the party' but I leave it be for now. She means well, even if she has a way of saying the wrong thing all the time. She's still the one I call when things go wrong.

My big sister. Protector and tormentor.

"Do you think moving here was a mistake?" I ask as I grab the wineglass from the little coffee table. I clutch it close like it's a life vest and I'm floating in the ocean. Foolishly, I wish I had a silly straw so I wouldn't even have to raise it to my lips. I could just tilt down, make my chin look all ridiculous as it meets my neck and sip through the loopy-loops.

You know, really lean into the patheticness.

I can almost hear Krista's shrug through the phone. "Maybe," she says. "But it's a good one. A spectacular one."

"That doesn't make it better."

"It makes it more fun, though," she says.

And maybe she's right.

Packing up my car and moving across the country to a town where I knew no one and had no job certainly was... Well, it was what Krista called '*a choice*'.

If I did move back home, it'd be a good story, at least. Even if everyone secretly thought I was an idiot for even trying.

"Look, everyone else at that dumb office can go suck it," Krista says after her long pause. The protective big sister in her comes out at last.

Her defense of me helps. Especially considering she got me the job. Or, at least, called in a few favors to get me an interview.

She sighs again. "Will you be alright tonight? Maybe just go to bed and work on cleaning up in the morning."

I throw my head back on the couch and a bit of wine splashes on my shirt. I am so annoyed at myself for spilling. Just one more thing to worry about. But I'm not annoyed enough to do anything about it. So the shirt is stained now. So what? Everything else is falling apart. "Yeah," I say. "I'll be fine. I'll clean up in the morning."

It's a lie. I can't leave all this out through the night. And I think she knows it too because she says, "Alright, well, let me know when you do go to bed. Text me."

"Yeah. I will."

This is a lie too. I'll probably forget.

"Hey," I call out through the phone, too loudly. "I love you."

"Love you too, weirdo," she says with a laugh.

Her little dig, the silliness in her voice, makes me laugh too, but she's already hung up.

I do feel better. At least, a little. I'm glad I called her.

Still, as I look around the room, I can't help but notice that I wasted a half hour complaining to her when I really should have been cleaning up. I have to at least put away the food or it'll smell in the morning. I can already tell I'll be hungover. I don't need to add stale bread and room temperature deviled eggs to the mix.

I glare at the platters on the little coffee table. Who even makes deviled eggs for a holiday party?

It's the least festive of the foods. I had added a little cilantro leaf and three pomegranate seeds to each half egg, though. The video I watched said the colors and flavors were a 'cute holiday touch'.

Greg said he thought cilantro tasted like soap.

Fucking Greg.

The old cushions under me sag as I push myself up from the couch at last. No time to waste. The cheap wine burns my throat as I drink the rest of the cup quickly.

A little motivation to keep going.

I shout at my phone to play Michael Bublé's Christmas playlist, and I get to work.

CHAPTER 2

At Least There's Donuts

The sun is rising as I set a terrible pace for my morning run. Honestly, I'm just glad I'm out here at all. I'm hungover, and it's absolutely freezing.

But once a therapist told me to go for a silly little run for my silly little mental health and, as annoying as it sounds, it has become a constant in my life. A way to clear my head. Something to make me feel like I'm being productive.

Even when my apartment is still a mess and I drank too much and didn't even get laid.

My breath comes out in a fog in front of me and I do my best to keep breathing through the stitch forming in my side just as the music in my headphones stops, replaced by the blaring of an incoming text.

Then another.

Then another.

Ben: Hey still on for coffee?

Ben: I've been here for a while.

Ben: Hey, I'm going to head out.

Oh fuck. My heart starts beating faster than the cold run could induce.

I completely forgot about the date. I scramble to answer.

Me: No wait! Be there in 10

Me: Sorry 🙈

The bubbles on the screen light up as he types back.

My face flushes as fog from my lips obscures the screen. I'm breathing heavier. Why am I so anxious?

Yes, he was super hot in the photos, but I've been semi-catfished before. Besides, it's a first date. He could be a serial killer. I need to chill out.

The phone dings again, too loud in my headphones. I look around me, trying to get an idea of where exactly I am and how much of my 10 minutes was a complete fabrication.

Ben: See you then

Me: Make it 15. Sorry. I will be there 🙈

Me: Get the apple spice donut. 😊 You wont regret it

Ben: Don't stand me up

His response is quick. And maybe fair. I'd be super annoyed if I was in his position.

My stomach sinks.

I can run there in 10 minutes. Probably. But then I'd be... *very* sweaty.

I weigh my options. What was it my sister always says? 'Over promise and under deliver'? No, I have that wrong. 'Under promise. Over deliver.' I've never been good at either promises or deliverables but I start a brisk walk anyway. No sense in killing minutes just thinking about the route. Slow movement forward is still movement.

I make it to the cafe in 13 minutes but I spend at least 30 seconds looking inside from a distance, trying to see if I can spot Ben and if my workout clothes look like 'hot girl on the town' or 'pizza rat in leggings'. But the image is obscured by the painted fake snow on the window.

There's no turning back now.

Dark green discount leggings and a black running jacket, hair pulled back, and what I hope is a cute flush in my cheeks will have to be what it will be. Maybe my confidence will make it all look purposeful.

I nearly laugh.

What confidence?

I can't even lie to myself.

I pull open the door to the shop before the second thoughts can stop me.

The bell chimes and a man in his early twenties looks up from his phone. He's sitting at a table close to the counter and, I notice, has only a black coffee in front of him.

No apple donut.

"Ben?"

"Annika?"

"Just Annie."

He smiles, creases forming in his chiseled cheeks and around his deep brown eyes. It makes him look a little older, but I like it. There's still a whimsy in his expression. His tousled black hair looks casual and effortless. It must have taken a while. Unless he has it down to a science by now, since all his photos sport the same style.

Still, a little of the product adds a sheen to his hair under the low hanging light above the table in a way that make him look... human. I try to give myself a little grace for my own disheveled appearance.

At least he's cute, even a little sexy.

I try to remember everything about him from our brief texts and his profile. He has a dog. A goldendoodle. And plays club volleyball.

I think?

Usually, I do more research.

I smile anyway and open my arms wide for a hug. "Thanks for waiting," I say as he stands.

Our hug is brief. I wish it lasted longer, if only so I could subtly do a sniff check and make sure I'm not post-run stinky.

"I almost didn't," he says as we both sit.

I look at the counter. The barista is busy with what looks like a complicated drink. I hope she's too busy to notice me getting scolded by this man about punctuality. A flash of indignation flares in my chest, but then again, he has a right to be a little annoyed with me; I suppose.

My gaze finds its way back to him, and I raise my brows. I don't know what to say. 'You're right' feels like he'd be winning some strange ground and any additional 'I'm sorry's don't feel right either.

I try to smile again. "Time is valuable, I get it," I finally manage. "No donut?" I try to change the subject quickly.

He looks down at his half cup of black coffee. "No, I'm Keto."

My frown hits my face before I can stop it. I need to course-correct. And fast. "I try to be healthy too. I just was on a run, so that's why..." I lean back in my chair and gesture to my outfit.

"So you forgot?" His tone is sharp. Sharper than his cute smile would indicate.

"Yeah, sorry," I fumble again. "I had a holiday party last night, so..."

He grunts, holds his coffee with both hands.

"It's hard to make friends here," I say, perhaps a bit awkwardly. My eyes drift back to the barista. I need a coffee. Sooner than later before I lose myself in my brain fog. "I just moved here a bit ago. Are you from here?"

"Born and raised," he says with no follow-up.

Cool. Great. This conversation is going well. *Why even agree to meet with me if you're going to be a jerk about it?* It's what I want to ask him. But instead I say, "This is my favorite coffee shop. Is it new?"

"I wouldn't know," he says.

My brows go up again. I want to shake him by the collar. "I thought you'd know, since, you know... 'born and raised'."

He smiles finally. "I don't come to this part of town often. Are you going to get a coffee?"

The legs of the chair scrape along the wood floor as I rise, a little too fast. "Yeah, much needed. Clearly." I try to laugh but it sounds very fake. I guess it is. "I'm getting a donut, too. If you want a bite. Call it a cheat day?"

He shakes his head. It looks like it's equal parts a 'no thank you' and disapproval.

I make my way to the counter and part of me hopes that when I turn around, he'll just be gone. It would be a merciful end to this disastrous date.

But, he's still there when I return. And I have to slink back to the table with my lavender latte and donut.

"What'd you order?" he asks as he raises a single brow at my cup.

I take a long sip, not caring that it is still too hot. I need caffeine. "Not Keto," I respond, cringing at my own words. I sigh and tap the ceramic mug with my fingertips. "So, you have a dog, right?"

"Yeah, a husky," he says.

Damn. I was wrong.

Then... who has the goldendoodle?

He takes his phone out of his pocket to show me his wallpaper. A smiling, blue-eyed dog stares back at me.

"Cutie! What's their name?"

"*His* name is Musk."

"Musky the husky!"

His eyes narrow.

I take another long drink just to shut myself up. This guy is giving me absolutely nothing, but I can't help myself. I try again. "Where'd you get him?" *Please be a rescue, please be a rescue,* I chant silently. *Give me literally anything to work with here...*

"A friend of mine is a breeder," he says as he types something on his phone.

I wait for a moment as he finishes whatever he's doing. Texting another date opportunity? Telling a friend a code word to call him and say there's been a terrible emergency and to come right away?

I should've done that. I need an escape.

"This... isn't going so well, is it?" The honest thought pours out of me before I can pull it back.

Ben shrugs, as though he doesn't care one way or the other and isn't even bothered by the point-blank question. Suddenly, he's opinionless. "It's fine," he manages to say at last.

I look down at my donut. At least there will be a tasty treat at the end of all this. He is really cute, but I just want this date to end. "I feel like we could go through the hour and the whole back-and-forth thing asking about favorite food places and workouts and then, at the end, dance around the fact that there's no chemistry. Or just call it now?"

He lets out a little grunt, a half chuckle. "I feel like *now* there's some chemistry."

The corner of my mouth twitches up. It's nice not to get a full rejection. But I've already made up my mind, and I hate the 'playing hard to get thing'. "It was nice meeting you, Ben. Good luck out there."

Ben's smile widens. He leans forward. "You sure?"

"Yep." Now more than before, I am.

I finish my drink in one big gulp, grab my donut, and head out of the cafe, leaving behind all the bad vibes.

So maybe my run was a dud today.

But at least there's donuts.

CHAPTER 3

Pieces of Flair Not Provided

My sister used to talk a lot about the 'Sunday scaries'. The feeling of dread people get when Monday looms over the evening.

I've never had that problem. Monday is future Annie's problem.

And then, of course, future Annie usually hurls curses through time at past Annie for being such an inconsiderate bitch.

Today is the same.

My alarm blares, and my eyes pry open like they're glued shut and made of sandpaper. I fumble for my phone, and already, I'm mad at my past self for staying up too late reading the latest in a dragon smut series. 'Just one more chapter' is the greatest lie I've ever told myself. And it's not even, like, *literature*.

I swear, groan, and roll out of bed all at once. There's not much time to complain when I wait until the last possible second to wake up.

My phone rumbles on the bathroom counter as I throw my hair into a high ponytail and swipe on some mascara.

Ben: Happy Monday

Ben: Been thinking about you since our date

I grimace as the words pop up on my screen. Let. It. Go. What's with these men becoming obsessed after being rejected? At least he's not calling me ugly and telling me I'll never find a high-value man like him.

Yet.

That's the usual reaction when I tell a guy I just don't see things going anywhere with them.

I turn my phone over to avoid looking at the messages and continue getting ready in a frenzy.

My nails click at the keyboard to log in at the front desk with less than a minute to spare before my official start time. From the long hallway to my left, my boss peeks his head out of his corner office and smiles at me.

I'm paid hourly, though I don't clock in or out. They pretty much take my word at 40 hours, though I figure it's best not to push the limits of the office's generosity, and I certainly don't want this reflecting negatively on my sister.

"Don't forget the music," he calls from down the hall.

I stifle the swear that is halfway out of my mouth and roll the wheely chair to the other side of the desk where the little CD player sits. It's old school, but it works, and the boss man loves himself some Christmas music. I brought my mix, which, blissfully, he allows me to play for the entire month of December.

After my years of customer service jobs, I think I'd rather jump off a cliff than listen to Mariah Carey ever again.

The music plays low, and I get to work on checking emails from the weekend on the slow-moving computer.

My phone dings again and I flinch, then fumble for it in my oversized purse.

Ben: I can take a hint

Hint? I was very upfront.

Ben: Good luck finding a high value man like me with a face like that

There it is.

Ben: bitch

Me: blocked

My heart is beating in my ears despite my best attempts to be nonchalant. This has happened more times than I can count– seemingly normal guys lashing out at the first 'no'. But it still gets to me every time.

I hate confrontation.

I sit up a little higher and look through the glass window into the open office space behind me. Greg is laughing with someone else, holding his coffee mug a bit too loose.

I sigh.

Maybe I should just settle.

I rise and get up to join them for a coffee break before the first five minutes of work has even begun.

The group looks at me like I'm an approaching swarm of

locusts. Except Greg, who does smile at me and offer a friendly greeting.

I do my best to smile back and grab a plain white mug casually.

Javi, an older man who has been working here longer than I'm sure anyone can remember, coughs a little. He's uncomfortable, but shouldn't be. I get why he wouldn't want to go to a studio apartment on the rougher side of town to attend a holiday party hosted by the new receptionist.

It's *them* I'm bothered by. Stacy, a man who acts like he's the center of the universe, and Lin, a woman who, despite her youth, has worked her way up. I eye them as I pour the coffee, but neither says anything about blowing me off, or asks me about my weekend.

I avert my gaze and focus on mixing in way too much vanilla creamer. I decide not to bother asking. Despite the boldness of coming all the way over here when the group lingers, I don't want to make people uncomfortable. I already had tons of gross tension from Ben's texts. I don't need to add to it.

"Monday, huh?" Greg offers with an entirely too hardy laugh.

"Yeah. Monday," I say back with a shrug.

Who knew small talk at the office could be so torturous. I should get some pieces of flair to pin to my lanyard. You know, really up the *Office Space* vibes. I'm sure they'd find a way to nag about that, too.

At least Stacy would. That guy really doesn't like me, or the way I add exclamation points 'needlessly' to every email. His words. Not mine.

Getting coffee was a mistake that no amount of sugar or caffeine can cure. I smile at the group, then motion back to my desk behind the large pane of glass. "Well, better get to it. Those emails aren't going to answer themselves," I say, a flimsy excuse for what I hope is office humor.

Greg and Javi chuckle, at least.

Inside, I want to curl up and expire.

I sit down at my desk, sip my coffee, and wonder for the millionth time if this is really it. No matter where I go, how far I run, it will always be the same.

CHAPTER 4
The Elf for the Shelf

The sun is already low in the sky when I arrive back at my apartment.

I'm tired. Well, I'm exhausted, actually. But I know it's my own doing. And that I'll make the same mistake again. Probably tonight even, if I'm being honest. I'll stay up too late reading books, vividly imagining I'm somewhere exciting, someone important. Getting boned by other exciting and important people.

I drag my feet across the parking lot and up the steep stairs to my third-floor studio. At least there's my vib. I should really name it at this point...

I perk up a little as I reach my door. A cute little red package with a green bow is sitting on my doorstep like a Christmas miracle.

Picking it up, though, I notice there's no sticker showing it's for me. No address, either mine or a return, is on it. I raise an eyebrow, and turn it over in my hands. It's small, about the size of my big purse, and as I flip it over, I hear nothing clanking around in it.

I right the package, hopeful that maybe it's some cookies, or some other sweet treat dropped off by a kind neighbor or ordered for me by someone who cares as I slip inside my studio.

The Christmas trees and string lights are all lit. I thought I turned them off before I left this morning. But, the place didn't burn down, and it's lovely to walk into, so I'm glad that past Annie is forgetful for once.

I sigh out what feels like the entire day's worth of tension and peel off my clothes, throwing my bra to the far wall like it's a bomb. I can finally breathe as I stretch my arms up and expand my ribs after being restrained all day.

Fresh undies, my fluffy robe, and knee high fuzzy socks later, I finally get to opening the package that has been sitting on my low coffee table.

The bow, it seems, is all that held it in place.

As soon as I untie it, the box falls open, revealing a very old-timey wooden Christmas elf doll. It's like an elf on a shelf, except, older, way less creepy, and yet...

I pull back, my brows rising in surprise as I examine the doll in my hands. It's worn, about the size of one of my old porcelain dolls I used to see in secondhand shops as a kid.

I try to place it in my memory as I inspect it. Perhaps Krista sent this? Was it one of ours as a kid and I just forgot about it? It certainly *looks* an heirloom.

The elf is wearing an all-red velvet suit and has a little striped hat that looks like one of those long nightcaps. His face and pointed ears are scuffed with time and wear, and as I turn him around, his limbs hang loose in my hand.

This is seriously weird. But at least it's kind of cute.

I close my robe tighter around myself and call my sister.

She's behind this somehow, but if it's an actual heirloom or some kind of prank to freak me out, I'm not sure.

"What's up?" She answers the phone and I can hear sizzling, popping in the background as she makes dinner.

"Hey," I say as I set the elf down and examine the box again. "Did you send me a weird little elf on a shelf?"

"Ew, no, those things creep me out," she says. Her voice gets farther away as she puts me on speakerphone. "Why?"

There's nothing on the box. No hidden address. No label. No note. Nothing.

"Someone sent me an old wooden elf doll. Or," I think aloud. "Someone delivered this here to the wrong address." I glance at the front door as my stomach drops. I really can't handle anyone knocking on the door looking for this thing right now. It's been a long day and I don't want to deal with a stranger.

I hurry to turn off my porch light like a coward.

"Weird," Krista says.

"Should I put it back outside?"

I can almost hear her shrug. The sound of her sauteing something in the background muffles her huff. "Does it look expensive?"

Picking up the doll again, this time more gently, I hold it close to my face. The woodwork is truly remarkable, smooth, polished, and vintage. "It's heavy..."

"That means it's expensive. Put it down," she quotes Jurassic Park and I laugh despite the budding anxiety. Another loud pop of the hot oil and she hisses a curse under her breath before going on, "I would keep it for the night. Put like a flyer or something in the laundry space or give it to the front desk in the morning."

"Yeah," I agree, setting it back beside the box for now. "Will do."

"Ugh, I can't believe you thought I'd send you an Elf on a Shelf." There's another, louder popping sound, and she screeches dramatically. "My bacon! I gotta go!"

My stomach rumbles. Brinner sounds delicious.

But none of the breakfast places will be open... I'll have to resort to microwave egg rolls like a goblin.

CHAPTER 5

The North Pole

You know those dreams where you're just walking and all of the sudden, there's this feeling of being dropped? Or when you're trying to fall asleep but your body jerks like you've tripped over your own feet?

I fucking *hate* that feeling.

I startle up, my heart already lodging in my throat and ears ringing. The blankets beneath me are warm, but the air is crisper than usual, like I left the window open or something... I blink, catching my breath as I sit up straighter, looking toward the window that... isn't there.

My eyes widen, heart falling from my throat into the pit of my stomach as I take in the unfamiliar room, the feeling of soft fur blankets cradling my body, and the chill on my exposed chest.

With quick hands, I gather my robe back up around my body, legs already scrambling back in the strange bed until I hit the heavy wood headboard.

Where the hell am I? Am I still dreaming?

My breath hitches as I take in the large room but my eyes

are a little blurry from sleep still so I focus my attention on the massive sleigh bed I'm in. It's like two king beds were pushed together, almost comically large, and covered in several layers of thick blankets. Some have white fur, others are velvet comforters, a chunky-knit green quilt... red velvet and silk pillows are scattered around me as if to cocoon me.

It's all so soft, luxurious, even cozy.

And yet, I'm terrified.

The room is spacious; despite the enormous bed, it hardly makes a dent in the usable space in the room.

Peeking up over the large sleigh footboard, I can see the dark wood floor covered in plush deep scarlet and forest green rugs. The walls are also a dark wood, seamlessly blending into the floor.

But despite all the dark, it's bright here. Several dangling glass lanterns that hang low from rafters light the space in a twinkling glow. It reminds me of the fairy lights I hung from my ceiling back home, except these are actual fires, and the light they cast is comforting, not a sad attempt at holiday spirit. Shimmering gold sconces along the wall flicker with warm firelight.

From the ceiling and around the perimeter of the room, deep green garland adorned with ruby red berries hangs in carefully placed formations. I squint at the closest hanging vines. They appear to be real, fresh, and smell of crisp fir and cedar. A faint trace of cinnamon wafts into the room as though someone just poured a cup of homemade hot chai.

It certainly doesn't *look* like I was kidnaped and placed in a murder dungeon. So... this must still be a dream.

Right?

I curl my legs in and up under my robe, but my fists at my side tighten too. Just in case.

It may be a dream, but I still don't intend to get hurt in it if I can fight my way out instead. Fear of confrontation be damned. I'm more afraid of being murdered .

At the far end of the room, the large, heavy door opens slightly, and the warm scent of chocolate and spices intensifies as a large man enters, carrying a golden tray with a steaming ceramic cup sitting atop.

He smiles at me kindly, stopping in the doorway when he notices me looking at him. He's... massive. His head nearly reaches the top of the door and he takes up all the space between the frame, with broad shoulders and a firm stance. His thick arms look as though they're about to burst the seams of the structured jacket as he holds the tray. Honey-colored hair falls into his round, dark eyes, and as his smile grows, so do the lines on his cheeks, leading down to his chiseled jaw.

I scan up from his full lips to high cheekbones and dark brows, settling once again on his eyes. There's a shimmer there, a light within that, despite my confusion, makes me feel at ease.

At least a little.

"Oh, good, you're awake," he says as he glances down at the tray and the steaming cup. He lifts it up halfway like he's offering it to me but is also a little worried I might spring up and attack him. Still, his smile remains warm. "Hot chocolate?"

It's a peace offering, it seems.

If he intends to harm me– I'd be shocked. But maybe that's the point?

I raise a brow at him. Somehow, with either his kind expression or the cozy smell of spices and pine, the fear is lessened. "Is there anything in it?" I ask as the smart part of me, the part who listens to true crime podcasts, finally kicks back in.

He cocks his head, a little of his golden hair falls further along his brow. "Cinnamon and nutmeg," he says, unsure as to the reasoning behind my question.

He seems genuine, but would he admit if the hot chocolate was drugged? I can't imagine many serial killers would get far if they were so honest.

He approaches, his warm smile returning as he balances the drink on the tray carefully.

"Where am I?" I ask, inching away from him slowly along the headboard.

He sets the tray down on the dark wooden nightstand with a little clanking sound, as though he fumbled at the last moment.

He is close now.

I can smell the comforting scent of cinnamon and nutmeg rising from the steam. It's the familiar spice of dark nights nuzzled under a blanket in the dead of a cold winter. And... something else.

He tilts his head again, and the smell is stronger, a deep and earthy musk like an expensive cologne pulsing from the defined line that runs along the curve of his neck.

"You're in the North Pole," he says. As though that was obvious.

I blink. My eyes dart around the room again, taking it all in. All the subtle, elegant hints of Christmas. Nothing like my studio apartment with discount fairy lights and plastic ornaments. Even the massive bed is a fucking sleigh bed.

I half expect a reindeer to emerge with bells on its harness.

This is a seriously wild dream.

"Are you hungry?" the man asks. And now that he's close, I can see he's got to be well over six feet. He's the tallest man I've ever seen. He tucks a lock of hair behind one ear, and I pull back further. His ear is pointed, long... like what I've seen in fan art of those fae romance novels.

Not that I read those.

That much.

"The... North... Pole?" I stammer over my words, unsure what I should say but hopeful I'll wake up from this strange dream soon. "Why... where–?"

He interrupts me with the raising of one hand. "Hot chocolate first," he says kindly. "I'll see about getting you something to eat."

I glance at the mug, then back to him. "I'm a vegetarian. Mostly," I say quickly, almost out of habit. Now that I think about it, I am starving. But not so much that I think I'd eat meat. Still, I don't want to be tempted if I can help it. Even in a dream. Maybe especially so. Dream bacon feels like a slippery slope.

He raises a dark brow. "No ham?"

"Especially not ham."

He lets out a small snort, amused.

I can't tell if he's teasing me or genuinely confused. But it irks me. I clench my jaw.

"No ham," he says with both hands raised in surrender. "That one is hard to import anyway."

"Even with Santa's sleigh?"

"Especially so," he says with a small, deep chuckle. "There's new clothes for you in the chest there." He points to the far wall where a large, heavy-looking chest waits. The wood is carved in elegant spirals and detailed carpentry work. "I'll knock before I come back, but you should have time to make yourself comfortable."

"Okay..." I say as I close my robe around me tighter, realizing just how exposed I am right now. Where ease, and even a little playfulness, once was is swiftly replaced by fear. It bubbles up in my stomach, and I close my mouth hard, afraid it will spill from me in a scream or sickness.

Where the hell am I, actually? How did I get here? *What... I think as my hands turn to ice at the tips, rushing cold through me, does he intend to do with me?*

As soon as the door clicks shut, I launch myself from the bed and to the chest. If he *was* telling the truth about the new wardrobe, I would at least like new clothes while I'm making a mad escape.

It'll be hard to run in a robe and fuzzy socks.

I push open the chest, finding it heavier than I expected. The wood is well carved, beautifully polished, and, as my sister would say, expensive. It is full to nearly bursting with rich, colorful velvets and heavy natural fiber pieces. I dig through them, looking for pants or a jacket with pockets, anything that would be *practical*.

But I find it devoid of practicality.

Instead, I shift through layers and layers of heavy floor-length dresses, each with warm collars and sleeves down to the wrists. None with pockets.

I growl under my breath. Under different circumstances, this would be a dream come true. Each piece is gorgeous and weirdly complements my complexion, and looks like it would fit me perfectly.

This could still be a dream, *right*?

Ignoring the swirling questions that flood my mind, I pull

out a dark blue dress and throw it on quickly, crumbling my robe and socks in the chest. There are little slippers in the corner, tucked into a velvet pocket along the side of the chest.

They're the same blue as the dress, deep as the ocean, and shimmering like moonlight hitting the surface. The soles of the slippers are a kind of wood, I think. They're thick, at least. I probably won't slip and slide around the floor like I would with just my socks, and the good news is: once I make it outside, at least I won't stub my toe on a rock.

The final girl always trips over a damn rock or branch or something. I'd like to not cut it close like that.

All dressed and ready to fight my way out, or at least make a mad dash for it, I hurry with feet as quiet as I can to the door again. I press my ear to the door, and hear nothing. But that could be because the wood is thick. Everything in here is made of the same dark, thick wood, it seems.

At least it's consistent.

The sound of the door along the floor hisses as I pry it open an inch to peek out. The hall is well-lit, but I still can't see much from the narrow slit. It seems to be the same decor as the room, so at least I'm not in a creepy backrooms.

It must be an old-time mansion...

I give up trying to see and instead I turn my head so my ear sits along the crack in the door. I wait, the sound of my heart-beat in my ears keeping me company. I count the quick beats.

One.

Two.

Three...

Footsteps approach. More than one person, from the sounds of it. They pause close to the door and I clasp a hand over my mouth to keep the sudden intake of breath locked away.

I breathe out steadily through my nose.

"What do you mean she doesn't eat meat?" a stern voice asks. Or, more like demands.

"She said she won't eat ham, especially," the voice I recognize as the man, or elf, or whatever he is, from earlier says.

"What about prosciutto?" the second voice asks.

A small sigh. "I suspect it falls under the same category."

"Shame," the second voice says.

There's a pause. A long one. *Too long,* I think, then wince at my own cliché thought. As if that were any part of my problems. My own inner critic is a bitch.

"She's listening," the second voice says.

Fuck.

I scramble backwards, looking around me for anything I can use to defend myself. My eyes land on the tray, the hot cup of chocolate.

It'll have to do.

I grab the tray with one hand, and hold the mug in the other. My limbs twitch with anticipation. I don't exactly have an exit strategy here.

But as soon as the door opens, and the two men walk through, I find my arm hurling the mug as hard as I can.

A loud burst fills the space as it explodes into tiny shards along the wall, coating it in a deep brown liquid that shimmers in the firelight.

The first man looks down at the shattered mug. His expression looks a little sad, with his brows knit and the corners of his lips twitching down. But it only lasts a moment. He smiles quickly and pulls the tray of greens closer to his body as if defending it.

My chest rises and falls quickly, from the exertion of racing to the 'weapons' and the strength with which I threw the mug. I hold the tray higher like a shield. "Don't come in here," I say. "You promised to knock."

He lets out a little laugh, and his eyes find their way back to mine. "You're strong," he says, amused.

From behind him, another man, just as tall and broad, pushes past him.

His hair, black and cropped short along the sides so they show off his ears more readily the first, shines as his head tilts slightly as he inspects me. His expression is also harder than the first. His chin and cheekbones are so sharply defined he could be a model. And as he looks me over, the muscles in his jaw twitch. His eyes are icy and impassive– as if he doesn't care about me, the tray in my hand, or the shattered mug beside him at all.

If I weren't so confused, I'd be star-struck. The first man is handsome, in a symmetrical, crush on your older sibling's best friend kind of way. This guy? He could get whatever he wanted wherever he went with a wink and smile. Not that he seems like the super smiley type...

He crosses his arms over his chest, his rolled-up sleeves of a white dress shirt exposing thick forearms and corded muscles that ripple as he widens his stance. "You're the one?" he asks me.

As if I know.

"She is," the first says. He closes the space between us with purposeful steps and sets the new tray down, not bothering to avoid me, or even really look at me too long, though the metal in my hand is still raised high.

I consider bashing him along the head with it as he moves the plate around on the nightstand, busy, it seems, trying to make the pile of green vegetables look more appealing.

But now that he's close, and I'm standing up, I see that it would be a futile hit. He said I was strong, and I am, but I'm not exactly a badass. And there's no sense in pretending otherwise. I am small, and they are both very large. My first hit would have to be not just good, but *the best* I can muster. And then I'd have to get past the dark-haired one blocking the door. But he doesn't look easy...

As my stomach betrays me with a low rumble, I know I'm not at my best. There's no sense in whacking him over the head just to piss him off.

The first looks up at me and smiles wide, the corners of his eyes crinkle. That bright light I saw in him before shines through infuriatingly.

It would be much easier to hate him and not slip into full Stockholm syndrome right away.

"I hope this will satisfy you," he says as he backs away slowly, not turning his back to me.

My eyes flash to the food, then back to the two men standing between me and the door. "This is a dream," I ask, though it sounds more like a desperate statement, even to me. "Right?"

The dark-haired one rolls his eyes. He releases his arms, dropping them to his sides, exasperated already with me.

"Oh, sorry I'm bothering you with my questions." Sarcasm drips from my lips as I finally lower the tray. My grip on it is so still tight it hurts my fingers. "I'm sure it must be so tiring *kidnapping* someone. My bad."

The dark-haired one side-eyes his partner. "She's a feisty one," he says, as if I'm not literally right in the room with them.

The other shrugs gently. "She has every right to be, Soren."

"I'm right here," I snap.

"You're right where you need to be," Soren, presumably, looks back at me. Truly, at me. It sends a chill rushing down my back and up my scalp. "Where you *want* to be."

I shake my head. "No, I want to go home."

The first lets out a small sigh. "Did you even taste any of the hot chocolate?"

My brows furrow. "No."

He shakes his head sadly. "I'll make another batch."

"I don't want it," I blurt. And it's true. Though, some strange part of me feels kind of bad about it. I shouldn't. But I do.

"Can we skip to the part where she accepts her destiny and that she came here willingly?" Soren asks.

"It's only a matter of time."

This is infuriating. I feel like a child. And worse, a part of me actually wants to start screaming and stomping my feet in a tantrum until they listen to me. I stifle the feeling down with a deep breath in until my belly is full. I exhale slowly.

Soren looks me up and down, his stare penetrating. Then, as silently as he arrived, he turns on his heel and leaves.

The other looks down at the mess along the wall and on the floor. "I'll be back to tidy this in the morning," he says, as if I would have the urge to do it myself. "Eat, and try to get some rest. I will explain everything when the sky is full of color." He moves to leave, and I find myself compelled to speak.

"Wait," I call out to him before I can force the words back down.

He turns, half way. One hand rests on the frame of the door, long fingers flex as he holds a powerful grasp on the wood. But he stays quiet.

"What's your name?" I ask, this time, my voice comes out quietly.

I don't know if it's because I want to know more about him or endear myself to him, but I ask it before I know what else to say.

The corners of his mouth turn up slowly, calmly. "Vetle," he says with a gentle nod of his head.

And just like that, he slips from view as the door behind him shuts with a soft sound.

CHAPTER 6

No, but Seriously, The North Pole

I have seen some seriously angry-looking bunnies in my days at the animal shelter. You'd be surprised at how pissed off a fluffy, chubby-cheeked little creature can be. Some of them would just stare at me, eyes narrowed, noses scrunched, quickly disappearing lettuce leaves, munching the green into their mouths like they wished it was your fingers instead.

That, unfortunately, is what I imagine I must have looked like eating the vegetables provided to me. I was starving, and, frankly, I had no idea how long I'd been asleep when I was spirited away from my home.

It could've been a while. A day, maybe two, judging by the intensity of the hunger pangs.

I decided it was worth the risk of poison, eventually.

But I *wasn't* happy about it and I ate with ferocity, angry eyes glaring at the door.

Now, with the plate clean and significantly less hangry, I wandered about the large room.

My eyes searched the tall ceilings, studying the holly leaf

garland and the rafters. Was there a secret, tiny camera hidden in here? Were those pointy-eared maniacs laughing about me and my grumpy salad and veggies as I ate?

The idea sours my stomach. Or maybe it was all the tomatoes.

With no cameras that I can see at least, in view, I turn my search to the floor. I crawl around the baseboards like I'm in that creepy short story I had to read back in high school. What was it? The wallpaper was some weird color or something, and the main character just crept about the walls until the wallpaper faded, slowly going insane.

I shiver to myself, then decide I still have my dignity. Even if it doesn't look like it. I don't seem to be in any immediate danger. No need to crawl around freaking myself out.

I move back to the bed and find that I'm more tired than I would have thought, given the circumstances. Vaguely, I wonder if there are pajamas in the chest. But before I have time to consider changing, my head hits the pillow, and I feel my body relax into the surrounding plushness.

I drift away, hoping that when I wake up, it will all have been a very strange dream.

I wake with a startle, warmth around me soothing my racing heart. It surrounds me, comfortably heavy. But then, the dip at the edge of the bed pulls me back to my surroundings. I live alone, but I am not alone.

With blurry eyes, I blink at the person-shaped figure near me.

Vetle.

He has positioned himself at the end of the bed, confined to the corner as though I was a dangerous animal he was trying to befriend slowly.

I sit up, pull my legs up close to me, and glare at him. If this is a dream, it's an awfully long one. I'm starting to believe that perhaps this is not a dream at all and I have truly been taken from my home. "Where am I?" I ask the question again.

"The North Pole," Vetle says with another flashing smile. "Did you sleep well?"

I shake my head, though the truth is, I slept better than I had in what felt like years. I feel refreshed, both in mind and body as the world moves into focus. "What do you mean, 'The North Pole'? Like... Santa Claus?"

Vetle laughs, the same warm sound that starts as a rumble in his throat and erupts out. "Well, not anymore, that's why you're here," he says at last.

My brows raise. "What?"

"Come for a walk with me," Vetle says, rising up from the bed, using his hands on his knees to push himself. He holds out a steady, large hand to me with the palm open.

I pull away but clamber over to the other side of the bed, rather ungracefully, in my long dress. Standing with my hands crossed over my chest, I narrow my eyes at him.

His hand lowers to his side. He waits.

I sigh, my posture and my will cave in. There's not much to be done, I suppose. At least if I go with him, I can get a better idea about my surroundings and maybe hatch an escape plan that isn't just 'throw mug then freeze'.

"Fine," I say. I come around to the other side of the bed with what I hope looks like steady feet and a confident expression. But I fear I may just come across as petulant. At least, from his bemused expression, I assume that must be how he sees me.

Still, without another word, he leads the way out of the room and I follow along like a shadow.

The hallway outside the door is long. Golden sconces line the walls casting warm shadows with their flickering light. A narrow rug, crimson and plush silences my footsteps as I gaze along the wall, looking for any hint of where we might truly be.

But at last, we leave the hallway, and enter an expansive common area. It looks like a traditional lodge-style hotel lobby, if I'm being honest. Heavy rafters loom overhead across the tall ceiling where a candle lit chandelier hangs.

Several large, plush couches face one another, each decorated with pillows and throw blankets. I lean in closer to look at them with a close eye. They look like those throw pillows you see at T.J. Maxx or Michael's. The ones with those scratchy fabrics and embroidered kitschy sayings.

Upon closer inspection, I think that's exactly what they are. One has fabric sewn 'Ho Ho Ho' and I spot another with 'Merry & Bright' in dramatic cursive stitching. Compared to everything else in the room that looks old, ornate, and expensive, these stick out painfully.

I cast a sideways glance at Vetle with a single raised brow.

He laughs again. "Like I said," he says, "Ham is imported. As are some Christmas decorations when we feel it needs some sprucing."

"Imported? From where?" A sudden anger rises in my throat before I can shove it back down. I sound furious by the question. And, in some ways, I suppose I am. I hate feeling like I don't understand something and he promised me answers.

"Come with me," he says casually, leading the way through

the large room and to a huge double door. He casts a playful smirk at me as I hurry close behind him.

I look up, up, at him. And scowl in return.

He pushes open one door and a blast of frigid air hits me in the face.

I pull back, my arms instinctually wrapping around myself tightly, trying to fend off the sudden drop in temperature. I blink, turning my body to see past Vetle and out into the dark sky, and brilliant snow, as far as the eye can see. A row of large fire-fueled lamps lines the path before us, the snow shimmering like diamonds, mirroring the starry sky above... and as I follow the stars, my mouth falls open.

The sky is on fire with bold turquoise and emerald, pink and orange. An array of lights falls from the sky like ribbons. It ignites the dark with gently flowing color, drifting like a slow current across the navy sky.

It catches my breath. I feel so small and... insignificant before this view.

"You see, Annika," he says gently as he gestures to the sky. "The North Pole."

"Just Annie," I breathe, then my eyes shift to him. "Wait, how do you know my name?"

His smile grows. "Come back from the cold," he says, noticing that my body is folding in on itself. He puts one muscular arm around my shoulders, and a swift warmth spreads from my arms up to my cheeks. "We have a lot to talk about."

CHAPTER 7

The Retirement Party

I am sitting on one of the couches with a warm mug in my hands, but the chill is still deep within my bones that no amount of hot chocolate seems to thaw.

I try again anyway, holding the mug close so the steam caresses my face gently.

Say what you will about being held captive, at least this is the best hot chocolate I have ever tasted. It is rich, just a little sweet, just a little spice that lingers on my tongue, an aftertaste of slight bitterness of real, good chocolate.

I feel mildly bad about throwing the first cup at the wall.

Only mildly, though.

"Run this by me again," I say as my eyes find Vetle again.

"You are at what I believe you might call 'home base' ... or 'Santa's Workshop' as the kids say." He chuckles lightly. He's sitting, casually, on the couch opposite mine. One leg is bent up, his ankle resting on his knee and his arms up over the backing.

Manspreading.

If we were on a bus, or at an airport, I'd be pissed. But on the couch alone, he simply looks like he is unafraid and unaffected by all of this. Like he's at home.

I look around again, up at the high rafters and the wreaths, the silly little pillows.

"Forgive the pillows," he says. "I admit, these are mine. I enjoy the less 'traditional' decorations. I like to freshen up the space every winter. Trade with the south is pretty easy, fortunately."

"South of the North Pole?"

"I suppose that's everywhere, isn't it?" Vetle shrugs. He leans forward, his legs unfolding as he rests his elbows on his knees. "You're here because you are the next chosen one. Our latest Santa and his wife are retiring. And we can't have a Christmas without the two."

I sip my hot chocolate slowly. I thought that was what he had said before. I'm tempted to ask him to tell me *again* but he was already patient enough to tell me twice.

I look up at his face. There's an etherealness of it, the symmetry feels almost unreal, and the long points of his ears only add to the sense that he's *truly* not from my world. Well, except for the red traditional elf suit that clings dangerously to his muscled arms and across his broad chest. He's lifted the sleeves up to the elbows to expose his forearms like it's a casual day at the office.

He's certainly unlike any Christmas elf I've ever seen.

"Why me?" I ask at last.

"You are chosen," he says simply.

I sigh, so hard that it's as though all the air from my lungs is gone. I crumble inward. "I want to go home." My voice comes out as a whimper. I wish it hadn't. I wish I sounded commanding and strong.

"I'm sorry, Annie," he says. His brows knit together, his face softens. He reaches one hand out to me but I pull away even though there's several feet distancing us. "But we need to develop your magic *here*. You are needed *here*. Without you, there won't be a Christmas. Now, or..." He looks down at his hands for a moment, then casts dark eyes at me. "Ever."

A frown etches harshly along my face and the wrinkle between my brows deepens. If my mother were here, she'd scold me and tell me I'll age prematurely if I keep making these faces. I nearly laugh at the idea. The absurdness of a thought like this popping into my mind as I sit before *an actual fucking elf* in *actually fucking the North Pole* is objectively ridiculous.

Vetle seems to notice my sudden change in expression. Though he smiles warmly, his head tilts a little, as if studying me.

"How long do I have to stay?" I ask. Then, my stomach drops. "What about my job?"

Vetle sits up straighter. "Your job?"

Ugh. He's right. How very capitalist of me. Still, I haven't so much as dared call out or taken any vacation since I got the gig. I didn't want my sister to look bad. How long will it even take her to notice I'm gone? "People will be looking for me," I say.

And they will. Eventually.

He shakes his head. "Time doesn't work here the way it does where you are from."

A dull ache begins to settle behind my eyes. I pinch the bridge of my nose with one hand, with the other, I pull the hot chocolate closer. "What... Do you mean? I need you to elaborate so so much." My hand falls. I look around the room as the feeling of suddenly being watched descends on me. "If this is... I can't believe I'm saying this," I grumble under my breath. "If this is Santa's workshop, where are all the... the um... other elves?"

"At the previous Santa's retirement party," he says.

"Retirement party?"

He nods. "Well, of course. He and the Misses have served us for 100 years. It deserves a celebration."

"100 years?"

I swear, I'm smart. I was a gifted kid in high school and everything. But I've been reduced to a parrot. He must think I'm an idiot. Though, to his credit, he doesn't show it.

Instead, he locks eyes with me and I'm forced to hold his gaze. There's something about the tenderness of his expression, the little creases at the corners of his eyes...

What am I doing? The guy looks like Dean Winchester in a freaking elf suit. And, despite the absurdity, warmth spreads quickly from my ears to my cheeks. I can't help it. I simply don't feel threatened by him. For whatever reason, I believe his kindness is real.

"Why aren't you there?" I ask, my voice comes out a whisper.

Vetle smiles as he leans back again. "I'm watching you."

"Bummer."

"Not at all, Annie."

My cheeks flush darker.

I pretend to be very interested in the contents of my mug, letting my dark hair fall around me so he can't tell that I blushed.

Stockholm Syndrome is one hell of a drug. As a kid, I thought Belle in *Beauty and the Beast* was a little too quick to accept her fate and here I am, blushing at a Christmas elf.

"Am I allowed to go?" I ask at last. "We could go to the retirement party together? It's a win-win. I could ask the old Clauses some questions. You could celebrate."

He rises, quicker than I would imagine given his stature. "Great idea."

Well, that was easy. Plus, moving about the place will help me to get a better sense of where I am. And, maybe get some more information. Though I shiver as I rise from the couch. I don't think I'll be escaping anytime soon. My dress is warm, but outside these walls is basically the tundra.

Part of me wonders if there's any polar bears out there. *Don't they hunt people?*

Vetle extends an arm to urge me forward, through the large room and toward an intricate door. Like everything else here, it is heavy and wood, and carved with smooth and strangely delicate detail work.

He cast a glance down at me. "Do you see these markings here?" His long fingers graze over the middle of the door where rune-like markings have been etched into the dark wood.

I squint at them, but they don't mean anything to me.

As his fingertips trace their outline, the etchings glow a warm gold, then transform to another series of markings I cannot read. "You will learn to use your magic like this," he says. His voice is soothing, a drop of honey in hot tea when your throat hurts.

I just witnessed magic. Or some kind of other trick that looked incredibly legit. And yet, my mind is not racing to discover what the secret is or how I am *here*, witnessing it. Instead, I let the scene wash over me as he opens the door to a ballroom where elves, all in red matching suits and dresses, move about the space with grace.

He guides me inside as my mouth falls open.

From the ceiling, crystal snowflakes hang as if... by magic. They capture the firelight from the chandelier and sconces, radiating out in brilliant warmth. Boughs of holly, dark green with red accents, line the room.

There must be at least a dozen people here, though I would have expected much more. At least, all the movies made it seem like there would be more elves. Though they are also supposed to be small. And not make me flush when they make unwavering, intense eye contact.

Vetle holds a hand to me. "A refill?" His body adjusts to lean closer to me, head tilted. He whispers, "It won't be as good. I didn't make this batch. But pretend it is, for their sake."

My cheeks ache, for the first time in what feels like a very long time, a real smile moves across my face. "I'll try," I say, handing him my mug. "Do you have any Baileys?" I'm not ashamed to admit that a little booze would definitely help the realization that I'm a socially anxious human among elves.

"Rum?" he offers.

I nod. "Just a splash."

"You pour," he says with a nod of his head for me to make my way deeper within the party. "Come with me."

I follow close behind, feeling strangely small among the tall elves. I glance up at a few of them as we move about the periphery of the party. No one seems to notice either of us and I'm grateful for it. But as the thought passes through my mind, a hard hand wraps around my wrist.

I yank back, hard, but to no avail. My hand is stuck.

"What is she doing here?"

I look up... and up.

Soren, the elf from earlier, with dark hair and knowing gray eyes has his gaze fixed on me, though the question was clearly directed at Vetle.

"Let me go," I hiss, pulling my arm again. This time, it comes free and he flexes his own hand as if I had just burned him.

His eyes move to Vetle.

"What?" Vetle says with a cheerful grin, his eyes bright. "You had your turn."

Soren's expression sours.

Great. So watching me has shifts. And not one anyone is clamoring to fulfill, apparently. Even though Vetle had made it sound like it wasn't *the worst*.

At least no one can hear us over the din of the room. It's a small party, but lively.

I sigh. My eyes trace over the faces around me. While I'm looking for this supposed Santa and Misses, part of me is still desperately trying to pull myself free from this dream that is swiftly turning into an anxiety nightmare. I look down, half expecting to be naked, stressed about missing a test as my teeth fall out. But no, I am still clothed, and Soren and Vetle seem to still be bickering with each other about who is on duty.

I step between them before I lose my nerve. "Please." Finally, my voice is firm. "I can look after myself. What am I going to do? Run into the snow? Start a fire in the corner?"

Soren raises a single brow at me. "Are you?"

"No!"

"You did throw a mug at us," Vetle says with a small shrug. He looks to the table at the far end of the room where a chocolate fountain flows, steaming, and so noticeable, I'm concerned about my powers of observation. How is this my first time seeing it? It's extremely obvious.

He turns back to Soren. "She can't leave the room without magic," he says quietly, as though I am not supposed to hear it.

Soren grumbles, folding his arms across his chest.

"Whatever." I push past Vetle, mug held aloft to make myself seem bigger. "I'm going to get a drink and meet Santa."

"Wait," Vetle says, reaching out.

I move to smack his hand away but instead, his fingers wrap around mine. A shock of his touch moves through me and my stomach drops. I look at his hand, huge around my own, and my heart sticks in my throat.

He, too, seems to have felt it. His eyes are wide and he drops my hand immediately. "Forgive me, I don't mean to move you. Just. Wait," he says in a low tone. "You're not supposed to be here. There's a process for this. Stay here, let me grab you a new drink, and I can escort you to your room."

"I don't want to go back to 'my room', it's not even mine!" I pull my arms around myself to avoid touching him again.

"Well, well, well..." A low growl sends a shiver through me. "Hello, future bride."

Ew. What?

Instinctively, I move closer to Vetle as a new man approaches from behind Soren. He's tall, broad, and... wearing all black except for a white and red striped Santa hat that's slipping from his head as he tilts to the side to get a better look at me.

Soren's eyes narrow but he turns to the new elf, his arms still crossed, posture still sturdy, though nonchalant.

"So this is the little misses?" The new elf says. He chuckles, adjusts his hat, so it's back on firmly.

To my annoyance, he's devilishly handsome. Who am I kidding? He's actually insanely hot. Dark stubble covers his strong chin, a noticeable difference between the other two who are clean shaven and put together. He smiles a cocky half grin at me, exposing a set of pearly teeth with a surprisingly sharp pointed canine. He stands with his weight on one leg, a slight sway in his stance.

So, he's a little drunk. Cool.

I decide I instantly hate him. He looks like all those men who know they're hot and wield it around like it's a sword, slicing the hearts of women like me. And I'm *not* doing an enemies to lovers thing. Been there, done that with enough overly confident men. The end is always the same. The fact that he's an elf doesn't change it.

Still, my words have escaped me. I find my mouth slightly open, about to protest, but nothing I can think to say is coming out.

"This is Annie," Vetle says as he gestures to me.

"And she's just leaving," Soren cuts in. He corrals me with his arm close to him and pushes me past the other elf. "My shift starts now."

CHAPTER 8

Cat is a Cat

"Who was that?" I ask as Soren guides me through the magical portal door.

"Aksel," he says gruffly. He leads the way back through the spacious lodge-like living room and down the same hallway Vetle and I had come from earlier.

I have to hurry my pace to keep up with him but he doesn't look back to see if I'm following or not. I glance at his ears, wondering if they can hear better than us, or if he's just so certain of himself that he *knows* I'll follow. Part of me wonders about kicking him in the back of the knee and running off. I'm not a fast runner, but I can outpace the average person.

But then, I run into the issue of being eaten alive by polar bears or freezing to death alone in the snow. Hell, I'd probably freeze before I got much farther than the front door.

I take another long stride, and I'm finally caught up with him. I look up, trying to read his expression. "Right, but *who* is he? Is he 'the Santa'?"

"He thinks so," Soren says.

"Hence the hat?"

He nods curtly.

I snort. He's giving me nothing. At least Vetle's a nice captor. "Are there more... like you around? The retirement party was kind of small."

"There are less and less these days," he says. His eyes flick down at me. "But none like me."

I raise a brow and look away. He's cocky, but there's a way he carries himself that makes it feel like it's at least warranted.

"That is to say, he's the warrior," a high-pitched voice sounds in my ear.

I jump, heart already pounding in my ribs. "What the fu–"

"Sorry to frighten you," the voice says again.

"Here we are," Soren says as he stops at the door of my bedroom. He is either ignoring or not hearing the creepy disembodied voice, but either way, being incredibly rude not to check in on me, I think, when I'm *clearly* in distress.

"Do you not hear that?" I nearly shriek.

He opens the door and escorts me inside, then closes the door gently behind him. "It's just Cat. Ignore her. I always do."

"It's true, he does," the voice says. From the door, the semi-translucent head of a massive cat appears. Its ears are pushed back, large teeth like those of a lion barred. Gray fur, thick and full, however, makes it look more like a Norwegian cat. Except. Massive. And see through? "Call me Cat," the cat says.

I fight the urge to flee since, well, there's nowhere to go.

Cat's head bobs to Soren, then back to me. "You have to invite me in," the cat's curiously little voice says.

"Like a vampire?" I blurt out, then think back to Aksel and his sharp teeth. "Wait, are there vampires, too?"

The corners of Soren's full lips turn up and I feel a rush of butterflies through my stomach. Did I just... make him smile?

"No vampires," Cat says, breaking me of my thoughts. "But rules are rules. Can you invite me in now before I become one with the door?"

My eyes dart between Soren and Cat. "Uh, yeah. Please come in, Cat."

Cat smiles, rows of sharp teeth exposed. "Thank you," she says, casting a narrowed gaze at Soren. She slips through the door, and closer to me.

She's huge. Her head is nearly level with me. She's furry, and fluffy, and if I was braver, I'd try to touch her but I'm paralyzed. With fear, or awe, or some combination of the two battling within me. She looks at me, her eyes up to my own. "Have you told her about the ceremony yet?" She asks, her eyes back on Soren.

"Ceremony?"

Soren stands tall by the door like a statue. He says nothing.

Cat stalks past me, sniffing at the pile of my old robe and fuzzy socks by the chest. She opens her mouth like she's smelled the worst thing in her life and a wave of embarrassment rushes through me. But she then looks at me kindly as though she hadn't just insulted my BO was pungent. "It's been a long time since we had to find our new Clauses," she says. "I'm sure Soren's forgotten. Just as he's forgotten to do the laundry." Her eyes flick back to the pile, then to him.

"Well," Soren says. "Go on, since you're so insistent on the sound of your own voice."

Cat grins, a human-like expression. "Someone needs to educate the girl," she says, almost sing-songy. She turns to me. "Perhaps it's best if you sit down for this part."

. . .

My head spins and I don't think I've heard even half of what Cat is saying because... I mean, she's a massive talking cat. Something about harnessing my magic, something about destiny and predetermined-ness... Oh, and apparently, I have to choose the next Santa. With the magic of true love.

"And... they retire? The Santas, I mean," I ask, cringing at my own question. It's really quite silly. They've established this already.

"Every 100 years," Cat says with a curt nod. "But that's a lot longer here."

"Right, time is moving differently..." I murmur. Fucking time dilation in Santa's Workshop. "Do we get time off? To see my family and...?" I want to say friends, but *ugh*. I haven't had many since moving across the country to chase a pipedream of making a new life. Anyone who was even vaguely friends with me before seemed pissed I left. As though I moved away from home *because* of them or something and not for my own reasons.

I ignore the sting in my chest at the thought that, really, the only people who would miss me are my sister, and my work. Or maybe not. Maybe my job will replace me within a day.

"Yes, you have plenty of time off to travel about, in the off seasons," Cat says.

I sigh.

"We call this part the Chestnut Trials," Cat says, moving on already. "It is where you choose the next Santa. Your debut will be tomorrow. You'll meet the old Santa and missus. They'll go off and enjoy retirement. Probably somewhere tropical. And then, it's just us."

I pinch my brow again. There doesn't seem to be any

fighting this, and if there was, the giant talking cat certainly killed it. I wave my hand, wishing I could summon a white flag.

I get to live for a long time, don't have to pay bills or fight with insurance companies, I get to see my family occasionally, and become magic? There's certainly worse deals. "Fine."

Soren raises a brow. "Fine?"

"Fine," I repeat, flopping down on the bed. I run my hand over the fuzzy blanket, and sigh the frustration out. "Fine, I'll do it."

Cat looks cocky. She becomes semi-translucent again and floats to Soren like a puff of smoke on the breeze. "Never leave a man to do a woman's job," she says with a laugh and disappears from sight.

"She's right, you know," I say, closing my eyes slowly.

"Yes, that's why we need the missus."

"At least you're aware."

CHAPTER 9

Mrs. Claus

The knock at the door startles me awake. For once here, I'd like to wake to the smell of fresh coffee and bird chirping. I'd like to wake up slow and comfortable.

The door is already half way open as I blink into the firelight, trying to see who it is.

A woman smiles at me brightly. I notice right away that her ears are like mine. A human, I assume. So, Mrs. Claus? But she looks so young, she's maybe in her thirties and looks happy, healthy.

She smiles when she notices me sitting up and staring at her. "I hope I didn't wake you, but I'm glad you're up," she says as she comes into the room on quiet feet. "My apologies for not making it to your quarters sooner. We had the party to plan and since then, I have been packing up for our journey. We are going to Australia first and I had to send one of the elves to get hot weather clothes. It was a whole to do, I fear."

She talks fast, but without a hint of nervousness in her tone. She simply sounds... excited. And as though moving quickly is her usual pace. She crosses the room and starts rummaging through the chest of clothes like it's hers. "I will send one of the elves to bring you an armoire. This chest simply will not do." She looks up when I don't say anything back. "Have you been to Australia?"

I shake my head.

"I am quite excited for the sunlight," she says. She's back to sorting through the clothes. She holds up a red dress with white cuffs. "Do you like this one?"

How... obvious.

I shake my head, though not at her question. Either of them. She hasn't given me time to respond. "I'm sorry, who are you? What are you doing here? Are you the old... um, former–"

"Oh, yes," she says. She rises again and brings the dress to the foot of the bed. "My name is Elisabet. I remember being in your position, though it was a long time ago. It can all be very confusing at first."

I lean forward in the bed. "Can you give me the low down?"

She tilts her head, golden earrings shimmer as they catch the firelight.

Oh, right. She's from 100 years ago. Or more. However the hell time works. I wonder if there's a TV here. Or books. If she knows any slang. I move on quickly. "Can you give me the quick details about what I am supposed to expect with all this?"

She smiles again. "Oh, yes. The trials are quick, or they were for me at least. I was able to harness the magic quickly and I fell in love with my Santa at first sight. Call it a Christmas miracle." She stands taller, tapping her chin lightly. "Though if I recall correctly, the one before me told me it took her quite a bit longer to choose hers and that her magic manifested sporadically." She shrugs one shoulder. "I think it all depends on you. The timeline, I mean." Her eyes scan me from head to toe, still buried beneath the heavy covers. "The first introduction is today, are you ready?"

Not even a little bit. "Honestly, can you just get me to a shower and a toothbrush please?"

"Ew," she whispers under her breath and a sudden shame rips through me, followed closely by anger. It's not my fault the North Pole sucks. "I'll give your guards a talking to. They should have shown you this the first night."

"In their defense, I did throw a mug of hot chocolate at them the first night..." I admit.

She laughs as she moves to the wall by the chest and pushes on it gently. "Oh, you're quite fun," she says as a hidden door swings open. "Here you are. All the amenities are the latest, I'm told."

"You don't get out much?" I ask.

She shakes her head. "No, there wasn't much left for me back home. The plague took most of what I knew from me before my arrival here. I was happier here."

I cast a downward glance at the floor. I don't want to ask which plague. Both to not retraumatize her and also because, at some point, it is starting to feel like the less details I have, the less confused I'll be. I manage a "I'm sorry" but I'm not sure how kind it sounds. I cringe at my own awkwardness.

Elisabet only smiles back. "Enjoy your shower and tooth-brushing. When you're ready, get dressed. I don't want to say we are all waiting on you, but... we are."

I pass her with a side glance and slip into the bathroom. I intend to take the longest shower ever and no amount of guilt tripping is going to stop me. I shut the door with my foot and for the first time in what feels like a long time, I smile.

The bathroom is massive, and warm. There's heat under the

tiles, warming my feet gently, and the huge shower is lined with rainwater shower heads. There's plenty of delightful smelling soaps, and plush towels rolled up in an open shelf as though it's a fancy hotel.

I slip out of my clothes and breathe in relief as the hot water hits my body. I scrub every part of my body, savoring the feeling of being finally fresh.

When I come out of the bathroom, clean from head to toe and with finally fresh breath, there's a small note on the dress, still at the foot of the bed. It reads, in neat handwriting, 'When you're ready. Wear this.'

Well, there's no fighting it anymore. I slip the dress on, comb through my hair with my fingers and decide that it's good enough. No makeup, nothing fancy. I tie my hair into a wet, low bun. These elves will just have to deal.

They're lucky I'm not wearing joggers.

I slip out the door and relief floods through me. There's no guard, no giant ghost cat, no Santa. As I make my way down the hall alone, I contemplate the situation I have found myself in.

Soren implied I wanted to be here. And, while I hate to admit it, there may be some truth to that. I wasn't happy, and that's why I moved away. I was running from nothing, and to nowhere. Just... a general sense of unhappiness. A sense that things weren't quite right with where I was even though I had nothing terrible to point to and nothing to blame.

So, perhaps, the truth of the matter is that I *was* unhappy and that this is all a dream and when I wake up, I'll find that I am still unhappy.

In a studio apartment.

With a crappy job.

And fucking Greg.

Who at least bought me Taco Bell once.

I do my best to banish the gloom that hangs over me as I near the door to the massive living space and resolve to at least make the best of this while I can. Maybe I can start making requests. More hot chocolate, first of all.

The room is full. There's way more elves than I would have thought, based on the numbers I witnessed at the retirement party. All heads turn to me as soon as I open the door and a strange silence fills the space.

In the center of the room stands who I can only assume is… well, Santa himself. He's next to Elisabet, holding her with a gentle hand around her waist. He's wearing the traditional red suit with white cuffs. Except, he isn't old, or round, or particularly even jolly looking. He kind of looks like just a generic handsome dude in his early forties. Still, his brown eyes sparkle as they land on me.

"Welcome!" His tone is joyous as he pulls Elisabet closer and raises a cup of what looks like champagne to me in a sort of toast.

Elisabet's smile widens and she snuggles up closer to his chest.

My brows furrow. I scan the room looking for Vetle, or Soren, or even Cat. But the only other pair of eyes I recognize in my quick search are the intense ones from Aksel. He's wearing the same smile as before and though I want to grimace back, my cheeks burn at his hard stare.

"Come in," the Santa calls as he gestures for the elves to move along so there's a sudden path to the center. "The first trial begins now."

"Now?" I ask, though I feel myself begin to walk toward them all as if compelled by some outside force. I look into the eyes of the elves around me as I move through the small crowd.

Elisabet nods. "It's best to develop your magic as soon as possible. And, choose the next Santa quickly."

"Right..." I start, then stop, mindful suddenly that anything else I am about to say will make me sound like an idiot. I have no idea what's going on, but at this point, I really may as well just accept it and move forward the best I can.

So, forward I go, until I'm up close and personal to Elisabet and her Santa.

For what it's worth, up close, they both seem even kinder and more whimsical than they did from across the room. They look delighted to see me, and even happier to be in each other's arms. After 100 years, I'd expect them to be like an old married couple.

Maybe the real magic is loving each other for so long.

I square my shoulders and look up at them. "Okay, what's the first trial?" I ask.

"Outside, there is a small flame," the Santa says. "Bring it back inside."

"That's it?"

"That's it," Elisabet and he say in unison.

I peer around them to the large double doors leading to the outside, then look down at my dress. "I don't think I'm dressed appropriately," I mumble.

"Your magic will keep you warm," Elisabet says with a gentle nod and two elves open the doors, letting in a blast of frigid air.

But I don't have magic yet... Isn't the point of the trails for me to earn it?

I grimace and pull back, wrapping my arms around myself quickly. It's instantly freezing in here and I call bullshit. They got the wrong person. I'm going to get hypothermia and die.

I look up at Elisabet who ushers me forward, and then my eyes land on Vetle, standing near the door, with a cheerful smile. What is he? Some kind of sadistic supervillain? He looks awfully happy about sending me to my demise.

I grind my teeth and squint past him to the outside darkness as I reluctantly approach.

The aurora is still ablaze in the sky above. The path of torch lights guides my gaze down the snowy path to a little flame, bright and bold despite the howling wind that now rages over the sound of my beating heart. I pass by Vetle and my scowl intensifies.

"Take this," he whispers. He shrugs off his own coat and wraps it around my shoulders, giving them a tight squeeze before he lets go.

"That's against the rules." I hear another voice say from behind me.

I pull the front of the coat around my chest like it's a life vest, knuckles turning white. I'm not letting it go.

"It won't help." It's Soren's voice now. "So it's not against any rule."

My stomach sinks and my nose goes numb.

"You can do it, Annie," Vetle says.

I nod and slip past the doors and into the icy wind.

It's like getting immediately slapped in the face with razor sharp icicles. I regret not drying my hair because I'm certain it's frozen to my head already. The ends of Vetle's coat beat around my calves and though I try to pull it tighter, I know I will let go soon. I can't hold it with winds like this.

I turn back to the lodge and my heart sinks low in my chest.

I've only walked a few feet and the waving of the elves behind me is no consolation.

Come on, Annie. You're a runner.

Run.

I throw off the coat and race toward the flame ahead, grateful that at least the snow is so tightly packed that I don't sink into it. But, still, it's running on ice and I slip painfully just when I'm within grasp of the little flame, flickering peacefully on the snowy ground.

I squint at it, at the shimmer of orange and red reflecting off the crystal snow. It's all by itself. Not contained or trapped, surrounded by glass. It's just a little flame.

All alone.

Like me.

I'm not sure what they expect me to do but all I know is I desperately want to grab any warmth I can. So I reach out, and take it.

The little flame doesn't burn, or even warm me really. It glows peacefully as I pull it close to my chest and turn back to the lodge. It's not so cold now. The wind isn't screeching in my ears. Maybe the magic is real. Maybe it's working.

I take a step forward, a smile crossing my lips.

And the world fades to black.

CHAPTER 10

One Bed

It's the sound of my own breathing that wakes me up. There's a warmth at my cheek, a snugness to my body that envelopes me completely. Did I make it back home through some strange portal?

I feel at home...

My eyes flutter open and I take in the storm around me still raging.

No, I am still here... in the snow. In the storm.

Then am I dying of hypothermia? I've heard it's warm like this. But there's a motion, a swaying of my body, swaddled close to something hard and warm.

I blink up to see Vetle looking forward with an uncharacteristically worried expression. His brows are furrowed, his jaw set tight as he carries me through the snow and back into the glow of the big room once again.

I close my eyes and find myself curling in closer to his broad chest, my cheek soaking in the warmth of his body as if he is the sun and I am feeling it for the first time. I close my eyes tight now. I don't want to see anyone else. I don't want to see stranger's stares, or disappointed gazes.

I just want to get warm again... And I fall back into a dreamless sleep.

The covers are piled on top of me, heavy. I nestle into them deeper, dipping my nose under the soft plush fabric. And that's when I notice it. The blankets are heavy, but heavier still, is the strong arm wrapped around me.

I am the tiniest spoon. And completely naked.

Electric tingles pulse through me, from my arm and waist where the skin touches mine. It shoots up to my scalp and my down to my toes, instantly igniting my once frigid core. My face is on fire.

I lift my head back out of the covers and turn slowly over my shoulder. As I do, the arm around me holds me closer, flushing my back to their hard chest. Fingertips curl just a little around my bare stomach to keep me from moving too much.

"You need to get warm," the voice says, low and soothing.

"Vetle? What–" I choke out. My voice catches in my throat before I can say anything else. The radiating heat from his arm and hands fills me. Yet, I prickle at the touch of his other hand as it rests on top of my head, stroking my hair. I want to ask what he's doing. Why we're here in bed, naked, or at least... mostly, but I find all words escape me as he gives me one final stroke through my still wet hair.

"You're not used to the cold, are you?" Vetle asks with a warm chuckle. He removes his hand from my head, but his other arm is still tight around me.

"N-no..." I manage. I turn my body over now to face him,

his hands find the small of my back and he runs one finger in a circle around the middle of my spine. "I'm from Arizona."

"Never been," he says. "I've heard it's a dry heat."

So they do get media up here.

I snort. "Something like that."

His honey colored eyes find mine and his full lips turn up. "I'm glad you're alright," he says gently. "But we need to make sure you stay that way. Just a little longer until your temperature is back to normal."

I swallow.

Normal. Right.

My entire body is on fire and yet, I do still feel the shivers in my limbs. I bite my bottom lip and curl into him, afraid of my eyes lingering any longer on his mouth, his easy smile, his eyes... "Am I..." I begin to ask before I can stop myself. I feel my shiver intensify. "Did I fail?"

A chuckle. "No, of course not. You're still the one. You'll complete the trials, obtain your magic, and choose our king. I have no doubt."

"You're optimistic."

He nods. "Always. Life is too short not to be."

"Even to an elf?"

"Life expands to make room for the time we have," he says. "This is my first time experiencing the trials. I'm excited to see how they go."

My shaking subsidies, if only a little. "How do I choose a–" I stop, noticing that the muscles in his arm tensed a little, tightening around me. My ears burn.

"You'll have your pick of the princes," he goes on. His head tilts so his chin is resting on the top of my head as if it was the most natural place for him to be.

I feel small. And cared for. Warm.

"You met one already," he says. "Aksel. There are two others."

"Is Soren one?" I ask.

He laughs. "No, we are lowly on the hierarchy. Guards, mostly. Occasionally... more."

I remember Cat's words. She had called Soren a warrior...

"Who knew the North Pole had guards and warriors," I manage to say quietly.

"It is needed," he says slowly. "On occasion. Like right now."

"Are you happy? Not being a prince?" The words tumble out of me before I can second guess. I feel strangely like there's a spark here, but he is also doing a job. I don't want to be a creepy patron hitting on a barista who's just practicing customer service.

He breathes in, deeply, his nose in my hair. "I am happy..." He pauses, then lifts his head again. "Are you?"

I close my eyes. "Only sometimes."

"That's a shame," he says quietly. "I think you will be happier here. Perhaps you've been unhappy because you knew you were meant for greater things."

"Maybe," I say.

We take a few deep breaths together, our bodies moving in unison, though he's so much bigger than me that his breathing is much slower. Matching him, I find myself calming.

I close my eyes and breathe in deeply, this time, on my own, surrounding myself with the smell of pine and fresh air, the hint of spicy cinnamon. He smells like Christmas. "This isn't like any Hallmark movie."

"I've only seen a few," he murmurs and pulls me closer so my breasts press into him.

I feel a rush of heat between my legs. I want to look up, to see if he's closed his eyes, if he's relaxed and calm as he sounds. But I stop myself for now. He's not one of my options here, I guess. And he seems content with that.

My brows furrow slightly. What the hell will I tell my sister when this is all said and done? The thought crosses my mind before I can stop it. But I don't want to think about anything right now. I just want to be.

And so, my hand finds the curve of muscle on his chest. With light fingers, I graze his skin, so softly that I almost hope he can't feel it. A sudden ripple of goosebumps textures his skin as my fingers trail down the line of his abs. I pull back, looking up quickly. "I'm sorry–"

His eyes, half closed, yet intensely penetrating, stop me. He tilts his head lower, his gaze rakes over my body, drenched in shadow beneath the blankets.

A wave of urgency washes over me. I bite my lower lip to stop myself from closing the distance between us, to stop from crashing into him the way I want to right now. My hands curl into loose fists and I pull them closer to myself.

What the hell is wrong with me?

"Don't be sorry," he says with his usual grin. "But it's probably best if I go now."

My ears burn.

With embarrassment, or lust, or idiocy. I'm not sure. I simply nod back and close my eyes tight so I don't have to see him leave my bed. Don't have to watch him walk away.

CHAPTER 11

100 Years of Avoidance

I wonder if I could avoid Vetle for the rest of my time here. All 100 years of it. When there's like... an extremely small elf population in what seems to be an extremely tiny village, that seems unlikely.

I want to thank him for saving my life, but I think a well written thank you card ought to do the trick. Maybe Rudolph can deliver it. Or Cat.

Wait, do they have a Rudolph?

I throw the covers over my head and wish I could call my sister now and tell her all about the most ridiculous predicament I managed to find myself in. Time moves differently here, they said. I wonder if a single hour has even passed back home.

A knock at the door jolts me from my wallowing.

"Come in," I call out. I'm not dressed, but what does it matter at this point? Besides, there's not a snowball's chance in hell I'm getting up anytime soon.

The door creaks open and I hear light footsteps cross the floor, then, feel the small dent at the foot of the bed as someone sits down.

A sigh. Then a light laugh. "Well, that didn't go how I thought it would," Elisabet says. "The old Santa and I are leaving soon. Usually we give you more details after you pass the first test. But..."

"But I failed."

"No, not at all," Elisabet says sweetly.

I peek out of the covers and watch her kind expression fall on me.

"I've heard it takes some newcomers several tries to complete the first trial. Of course, I did only take the one..." She trails off like she's reminiscing. "But I don't think that's typical." Creases form at the corners of her eyes. She's teasing me.

I try my best to smile back, but I'm sure my face looks unconvincing.

"Here's the thing, my love," she says. "You'll get your magic after the trials are complete. Then, you'll be able to choose the new Santa."

"From one of the princes?" I ask.

She nods. "Aksel, Geir, and Isak. You can't go wrong with any of them." She leans in a little, one eyebrow cocked. "But I'd pick Aksel, if I were you."

"Why's that?"

He seemed like a bit of a cocky drunk to me. But maybe I caught him at a bad time. I would hate to be judged from my over consumption at a holiday party.

"He's the most handsome," she says with a laugh and a wave of her hand. "Nothing more."

I snort.

"Oh, I know it's not all about looks," she says. "But it certainly helps. You'll feel the pull in you when you know the right one." She pauses for a while. "Do you believe in soulmates?"

"Not really."

My parents divorced, like so many in my generation. I have had a horrible string of dating in my adult life. I never gave much thought to the concept of a soulmate, but I guess if all this is possible, maybe soulmates are too.

"Some things are fated," she says, breaking my thoughts. "When you pick a prince, you'll find the connection is stronger than anything you can imagine. It will drive every decision you make. And he will be entirely devoted to you."

"That sounds nice," I admit. And it really does. I like the idea of never having to go on a terrible date ever again. Never having to swipe through a bunch of photos of dudes holding fish and sitting on cars and saying stupid things like 'I pay for dinner. I'm an alpha' or '6'2 in heels'.

I like the idea of all the hard work of getting to know someone be an instant lighting strike. Of not having to guess at if it's the right person or if things will work out. For whatever it's worth, at least Elisabet seems happy.

"It is nice," she says. She looks at the door and nods. "Our time is up. What else do you want to know before I go?"

Stupidly, I want to ask if there's reindeer. But I figure I'll find out soon enough. Instead, I ask, "How often do you get to go home?"

"As often as you'd like," she says. "Once the trials are complete. In the off seasons."

Calm descends over me. "And..."

She rises from the bed.

"Any other tips?" I blurt out.

"Trust yourself." She smiles and gives me one last nod

before she slips from the room and the door closes quietly behind her.

Trust yourself.

I always have. But being here has thrown me off center.

I mean, I just figured out that fucking Santa Claus is real. Trusting myself again is going to take some time.

My eyes drift up to the rafters and I breathe in deep.

Or, maybe I'm here, in part, because I never really trusted myself at all.

All I know now is that I'm hungry.

Before I can second guess, I throw off the blankets and find my crumbled dress on the floor. I slip into it and secure my feet into the somewhat uncomfortable wooden shoes, mentally noting that the first thing I'll ask for is a good set of running sneakers.

CHAPTER 12

The First Trial. Again

The doors open again and this time, I am already bracing for the cold.

I wish someone had told me before the first trial that:

1. I would be saved if I passed out from wind damage
2. Lots of other previous future Mrs. Clauses had failed the first few times

It makes this try much less daunting. Besides, I'm a runner. All I have to do is sprint out there as fast as I possibly can, and then sprint back, right?

While, you know, holding a magic fire. Easy.

As I move through the line of elves, though, this time, I do seek out several faces. Aksel, with his head slightly tilted, eyeing me like I'm a wonder, or a curiosity. Behind him, Soren looks disinterested. His eyes are narrowed on me as if he thinks this is all a massive waste of his time. I find Isak, his green eyes shining in the firelight.

70

Beside the open door, I look up at Vetle.

"I'll be there, if you need me," he whispers with a wink.

A warmth fills my core. It's not embarrassment, or shame like I would have thought. But instead, it's security. If I fall, if I don't make it, he'll come for me.

Despite my previous concerns, I feel my smile light my face. I ready my stance, feet planted to the ground, arms up. I narrow my eyes into the dark, though the torches and the sky still provide a surprising amount of light. I can see the little flame battling the cold out there in the snow.

The wind still rages, but I know what it feels like now.

I can do this.

I take in one final deep breath, filling my belly with air, and I shoot it out quickly as my legs propel me forward into the icy night.

Scooping up the flame is easy. This time, I don't second guess it. I don't question when it grows around me, when I feel warm as I race back to the safety of the elves and the warm room where familiar faces await me.

When my first foot crosses the threshold of the room, it's like an instant shock. The fire grows even brighter in my hands. It's warm. Not too hot.

Outside, the wind suddenly stops. The aurora burns brighter, illuminating the sky like dawn.

A few cheers erupt from inside, then, the fire flickers out, bursting from my hands to each sconce, illuminating the space with an even stronger glow.

I look down at my hands, then to the outside once more. Suddenly, it's not too cold anymore. Don't get me wrong, I'm still freezing. But the plummeting temperature like I've been dunked in ice water is rising, at least, to me.

"You did it!" Vetle says with a little fist pump that feels strangely out of place with his elf suit and pointed ears.

Pride fills my chest as I turn back to admire the icy landscape, now fully in view for the first time. I step back out, and no one stops me. The rows of torches that line the main path lead to what appears to be a few dotted trees out in the distance. I'm surprised I missed it the first time, though, in my defense, it was pitch dark and snowy wind obscured most of my vision. To the left and right, little houses that look like they're straight out of a fairy tale speckle the landscape.

"The first trial is complete," Geir's voice calls out and the cheers grow louder. "Our winters will be mild for another 100 years."

I turn back to the group. A mild winter, huh? I guess that feels magical...?

"Plus, you'll become more accustomed to the cold as your magic grows," Vetle says as he leans in a little for me to hear.

I look down at my hands. I already feel it– though I doubt I'll ever *truly* get used to it.

"Upon completion of the last two trials, the balance will be restored," Geir continues in his formal tone.

I roll my eyes.

Elisabet was onto something with her assertion about Aksel. Geir is far too much of a formal showman. It's nearly a parody of a sportscaster.

My scalp tingles when I feel a stare on me.

From across the room, Soren is watching me. From his wicked half smile, it's clear he saw my eye roll. And that he relates.

My smile widens to a laugh and I wrap an arm around myself as I move through the crowd and away from Geir who is still going on about the trials and the choices and how summer will be plentiful.

He's nice enough, it seems, but right now I just want to relish in the feeling of magic flowing through me. As I walk, I feel myself standing just a little taller.

No one seems to notice, or follow at least, as I leave the large room and down into the quiet hallway. I'm alone at last.

Except for Cat. Her massive head appears through the wall ahead of me. "Sven will owe me 15 sardines, so thank you for that," she says as the rest of her fluffy body moves through the wall to walk beside me.

I raise a brow at her.

"He thought it would take you at least five tries," Cat explains. "I called under. It was an easy bet."

"What would you owe him?" I ask. "If he had won?"

Cat's head tilts. "15 sardines. They're a delicacy."

"And... hard to come by? Don't the elves go to discount stores for decorations?"

Cat lets out a little puff of air, a sort of laugh. "It's more the spirit of the competition," she says. "We haven't had a lot of excitement in the last... many years."

"Got it. Well, I'm glad I could help."

We stop at my door where Cat is already starting to disappear.

"Hey, Cat," I say before she's entirely gone. "Do you think you can have one of the elves get me some running gear? And maybe headphones?"

Cat nods. "And how about more sardines? For a friend."

"And more sardines, sure."

"Well, if the Queen demands it," Cat purrs as she disappears from sight.

CHAPTER 13

Magical Side Effects Include Hunger and Horniness

I decide I've earned a bit more exploration. I am curious about the door that Vetle had shown me and want to try out my new magic there...

I stand before the door with a puzzled expression. I have absolutely no idea what these runes mean and I'm a little worried it'll be like an emergency exit and I'll set off an alarm if I touch it. Or, that I'll accidentally open a portal to somewhere scary.

But I'm starving, and so, I put my hand on the door, and the runes flicker, faintly. "To... food?" I ask aloud and the door swings open, revealing a kitchen that looks like it's owned by a chef and straight out of HGTV.

I step through the threshold and make my way inside, eyes wide.

The fridge is surprisingly high end. One of those massive double door ones they have in restaurant kitchens. It's stainless steel and free of any scratches, dents, or even fingerprint smudges. And, I mean, I didn't exactly expect them to even have a fridge. Every Christmas movie ever shows the elves with quaint little workshops.

Of course, those movies don't have elves... like these. Tall, surprisingly muscular when they hold you tightly under thick covers...

I open one of the doors to the fridge quickly, trying to shake away the thoughts of surprisingly sexy elves. I'm supposed to be learning magic. And passing the trials. And–

I stick my head all the way inside the fridge. But the feeling of the cold air hitting my face does nothing to cool down my body.

I shouldn't even be thinking about magic, right?

This whole thing is crazy.

I scan the contents of the fridge for something to eat. But even though I was starving a moment ago, this feels mostly out of boredom. And a little to satiate a hunger of a different kind building up in my core.

"Magic makes you hungry."

Soren.

I slam the door shut to see him standing close, arms folded over his chest, head slightly cocked.

"Congratulations, by the way," he adds as an afterthought.

"Thanks," I say dryly. But the way he's looking at me, like he's seeing me, *really* seeing me, sends a rush of warmth to the tip of my nose. I look away to avoid him noticing. "Why are you here?"

"I'm your guard," he says simply.

One brow quirks up, betraying my curiosity. I study the dark hardwood of the floor, trying to look disinterested. But I follow the grains as they travel until I reach the hem of his pants. "Are there dangers here that would require a guard?" I ask, my eyes trailing up his legs, over his chest where his arms are crossed. His dark red sleeves are rolled up to mid forearm, where it looks like he couldn't stretch the fabric any higher. His arms are thick, lines of defined muscle twitch as he moves under my stare. I find his eyes at last. Impenetrable, as usual. "Or are you keeping me from leaving?"

The same half smile flashes across his face. He tilts his head. "You wouldn't make it far. Even with your magic shielding you from the cold."

I take a step closer to him.

He stays where he is, same slightly amused expression, except... his stare hardens.

My heart is beating faster in my chest, I feel a tightness there, like I can't quite breathe in deeply. But still, I find myself taking another step closer, hand grazing the stainless steel island, half for support, half to just feel the chill of it on my skin, grounding me.

I'm close now and he still doesn't move. Instead, he tilts his head down, just a little, to see me better. I'm not short, by human standards, at least. But he's towering over me like a mountain. I can't get past him. And I don't think I want to. I want to be closer to him and I can't explain why.

"Why do I need guarding?" I ask again, my voice barely a whisper.

He unfolds his arms, puts one in his pocket, casually. His other hand lifts, nearly touching my chin but he won't move forward. His eyes darken and he lowers his head closer still. "I am here to protect you against anything that seeks to harm you." His fingertips graze my neck, just barely.

It's like a fire has burst within me. My heart pounds

beneath my dress. The feeling of falling in my stomach suddenly has me reeling.

His jaw tightens and he moves his hand away. "Even from me." Soren's voice is nearly an inaudible growl through gritted teeth.

My eyes move slowly over his face. I don't know what to make of what he just said, or of how he said, or the sense of emptiness I feel now that he steps away. "You would hurt me?" I ask at last.

A small chuckle escapes his throat. He takes another step back. "Only if you begged me to," he says at last, then turns away from me so quickly I'm almost not sure I heard him right. "Go back to your room," he says over his shoulder. "I'm on duty tonight. I'll bring you what you need."

My face is hot, my fingers tingle. I'm not sure I *could* walk away on these shaking legs. "Hot chocolate, please," I burst out. "And... something to eat."

My stomach is in knots, but I'm ravenous.

The moment with Soren has left me feeling like both an idiot and also way too hot and bothered. I don't understand what's gotten into me. I've never been like *this*. I'm not a prude or anything, but if I really just wanted sex, I'd be... well, fucking Greg.

I pace around my room for a while, trying to figure it all out. Maybe it's a side effect of the magic? Elisabet said something about soulmates. It could be the magic forcing me to find mine quickly.

Maybe I just need to take a nice long shower and... take care of it myself. Being horny is clogging my judgement. And I need to be clear headed. I have no idea what the other trials are going to be and though the first one was easy... ish, I still nearly got hypothermia.

Get it together, Annie. I scold myself as I stomp my way into the bathroom.

Turning the water to maximum heat, I wonder if Cat or the elves would go get me a vibrator. I laugh at the thought and slip out of my dress. Even the touch of it sliding off my skin is sending me over the edge.

Is the North Pole some kind of vortex or something? What the hell is this?

I step into the shower and curl up to let the water wash over me, turning my skin red under its droplets. All I can think about is Soren's words. His low, rumbling voice. The way his eyes held mine captive.

I slide one hand between my legs, finding the throbbing ache there and I gasp at the touch.

Another thought crosses my mind as my heart races even faster. It's Vetle. His arms around me, the heat of his body, the goosebumps on his skin as I touched him... I remember the way he touched me, drawing little circles around my back and running his hands through my hair.

Sparks fill me remembering Soren's touch on my neck...

I throw my head back. A climax rips through me, pulsing through every limb in waves of electric shock. I stifle the sound as best I can and hope that the water falling muffles it further.

Sitting in the shower as hot water cleans me, I can't help but let annoyance take hold. My little session helped, but not by much. I'm still left craving... and a little worried about what I'll do when Soren gets here with food and drinks.

I don't think I trust myself to be alone with him... or my other guard right now.

CHAPTER 14

Radioactive Hot Chocolate

The cup of hot chocolate is already lukewarm by the time I make it out of the shower. It rests on a wooden tray at the foot of my bed, along with a slice of cake, and what looks like every single berry variety on the planet piled in a cute ceramic bowl.

There's no note, no indication that Soren was here at all except for the tray of food.

I grab the drink first, taking a big gulp to satisfy my thirst. *Oh my god.* I gag on the hot chocolate wishing I hadn't just swallowed it. It is *really really* terrible hot cocoa. I swirl it in the mug, squinting at it. Did he make it without *any* sugar? And with pool water?

I cast a glance at the door as I set the mug down with a light thud on the tray. I really hope that it was Soren's hot chocolate I threw that first night. That would be doing a public service.

A smile crosses my face as I sit down beside the tray, still naked and thoroughly appreciating that I'm not cold at all so I can just slowly air-dry in peace. Beads of water drip down my back from my hair and normally, I'd be shivering, but I have to admit, I'm enjoying the new ability to stay warm.

I pop a strawberry into my mouth and savor the delicious, bright flavor. It's something else to focus on other than the idea that Soren was just here, right beside my bed. That he might have been listening to me in the shower...

Though, the disgusting drink does help lower him from the pedestal I put him on. At least when he annoys me now, I have this to fall back on. *Oh yeah? Well, you make terrible drinks and it's not even that hard to make hot chocolate.*

Ugh. I sound like a child.

I need to go for a run... I wonder how long it'll take them to bring me what I need. And if I even *can* run in the snow without slipping and sliding around.

I really hope the magic extends to my footwear.

Cake and berries finished, and hot chocolate safely dumped down the drain like the absolute biohazard it is, I finally dress and decide to try my hand at exploring the outside again. The little village looked adorable, and, frankly, I think I could use the Christmas cheer after everything.

I crack open my door, and both Soren and Vetle turn to me.

Vetle's smile brightens.

Soren grimaces.

I do my best to look regal. Queen-like. "I'm off to explore the outside," I say confidently.

"All fueled up?" Vetle asks as he holds out an arm, gesturing for me to start walking.

"Yep." I start walking down the hallway, my green dress trailing just a little behind me.

From behind, I hear Soren's deep voice. "Did you enjoy the hot chocolate?"

I stop, but don't look back. Is he asking because he poisoned it? Or because he's genuinely curious. Is he... anxious about it? I start my walk again. "It was..." I trail off, unsure how to respond in a way that doesn't hurt his feelings but also doesn't inspire him to use the same recipe.

"I told you to let me make it," Vetle whispers to Soren.

I can sense the other elf's posture tighten. He grumbles something under his breath I can't hear.

"The cake was good," I offer, somewhat apologetically.

"Thanks!" Vetle says, happily. "It's an old recipe, but a good one. I'll try to make you something with more protein next time. But the sugar helps ease the magic use."

I hum. Makes sense. Kind of. You know, sugarplums and candied nuts and all that. These traditions had to have come from somewhere. Or simply it was kids getting hyped up and parents just letting it happen for the sake of some semblance of harmony during the holidays. "Well," I say at last, "thank you for making it. And delivering it. As far as protein... I like chickpeas."

"Chickpeas?" Soren asks, mostly, it sounds like, to Vetle.

"What do you want to see in the village?" Vetle asks, louder. "I'm afraid there isn't much happening right now. We've been mostly preparing for the retirement and your arrival."

We enter the large living space and I stop. It's empty but it feels so much more.... public. *Good*.

"I want to see what there is to see," I explain. "I just got here and I only know this room, the dining room, the kitchen..." An image of Soren, sleeves rolled up, head cocked, standing tall with enough confidence for both of us flashes through my mind. "My bedroom–" Vetle, laying beside me, his lips nuzzled into my hair– "I need to go outside!" I nearly shout as I barrel forward. "Yep, outside. Fresh air. New things to see... I can find a running route."

"Running?" Vetle asks as he catches up to me.

I'm already at the door. "Yes, I asked Cat to help me get some gear."

"And Sardines," Cat says, her face appearing from through the door.

I jump back. "Cat!"

"Cat," both Soren and Vetle say, commiserating with me.

"They were delivered, by the way," Cat says, ignoring all of our shock.

"Already?"

Cat looks at me like an idiot, the way only a cat can. "Time moves differently, remember?"

I shrug. I am not sure I have the bandwidth to figure out the time space mechanics of *the North Pole* right now. Instead, I gesture for Cat to back away. "Alright, I'm glad you got your prize. Can I go through now?"

Cat disappears through the door again. "Of course," she says.

I reach for the door, but Vetle has beat me to it. His hand brushes over mine as he opens it for me with one wide swing and a big grin. "My Queen," he says, though there's the slightest hint of playfulness to his tone. Like he doesn't quite believe it.

Not yet, I think. But I keep it to myself.

The outside is lighter than it ever has been. The torches burn bright, and the swirling aurora casts a dawn-like cold light over the shimmering snow. I step out, grateful that it is just a little chilly rather than frigid, and look to each side of the long path.

Just as last time, there's scattered colorful wood structures. They look like cute little homes, though some have swinging signs hanging over their bright doors indicating a business of some kind.

As if this place was big enough to lose their way... It's the smallest village I've ever seen.

Unless I'm missing something.

Vetle stands beside me, his warmth radiates out.

I tilt my head up to him as he glances down.

"Why don't you let us be your tour guides?" He holds his arm out to me, bent at the elbow for me to take as though he's afraid I'll slip on the icy path.

I blush, but loop my arm in his anyway. I pull my gaze ahead. "Where to first?" I ask.

"Are you in the mood to meet anyone?"

The hairs on my neck stand up as Soren comes closer. He stays behind, as if he's in the secret service or something. I half expect to turn to him to see him raise a cuff to his mouth, speaking into a hidden mic attached to a clear earpiece.

"Not really," I say truthfully. I'm grateful for the question. Between, well... everything, I really just want to clear my head. Get a lay of the land.

"Then I'll take us to the outskirts, we can see everything better from the hill."

I look around, no hills in sight. I guess I'll just have to trust. "Let's go."

Vetle lets out a small chuckle. He leads me forward, with Soren close behind like a shadow.

Down the path, I keep my head on a swivel, trying to take

everything in. It's quaint and cute and as a few elves pass by, I can see there's so many more than who was at the retirement party and the celebration of completing the first trial. There's men, women. Some in long dresses like I wear, others in the familiar suits. But no children.

"How many people live here?" I ask, catching Vetle's dark eyes.

Vetle glances back to Soren. "Oh, probably close to 200. Is that right?"

I follow his stare to Soren, who merely shrugs.

Ugh. His nonchalance infuriates me.

I keep walking forward with Vetle. My eyes find the space where our arms are linked, the curve of his long fingers, gently folded inward beside my small hand. I change the subject to the least sexy thing I can think of. "Are there any children? Like, kid elves?"

Vetle shakes his head. "No," he says. "Not for a very long time."

I hum. I'm not sure what I expected. This is, after all, a magical place where time and weather and even the sky seem to work differently. My eyes scan the horizon as we near the end of the path. "Is there a Rudolph?"

Vetle laughs. "No, no Rudolph. We have the flying reindeer, though. The magic kind. Good question, though," he adds the last part quickly, though his laughter is still lingering in his tone.

We reach the end of the path, and ahead is all ice and snow, and a few dots of evergreen trees in the distance, though I'm certain those are also magical in some way. I'm not sure trees really grow here naturally.

Vetle guides me to turn around, and, somehow, we are up on a hill overlooking the village.

Has it really been uphill this whole way? It felt like nothing.

Still, the image of the little town has me filled with a sense of wonder. It glimmers with firelight and warmth. I can smell cinnamon and clove in the air, hear the sound of faint music, and a little laughter. It's like looking into a magical snow globe. It's as though the village is a miniature, and we are standing outside it, looking in. I decide not to ask how this is possible. There'd be no point. Instead, I release from the elf's strong hold and tuck my arms around my body gently.

Soren finishes his climb to stand at my other side. Between the two of them, I do have to admit, I feel safe. Warm. Protected.

The scene before us looks peaceful. Light. Happy.

No stupid customer service calls. No bills to pay. No bad dates...

The reality of it comes crashing down all at once. "I have to pick one of the princes...?" I ask, though my voice trails off, caught on the little breeze that blows tiny shimmering snowflakes through my hair.

"Yes," Soren says.

"When your magic manifests completely. After you pass the trials," Vetle adds gently. "You have time to decide."

Time. He says it like he understands. I haven't really spent any of it with any of the princes. And, frankly, I'm not sure I want to.

But it is just as that thought crosses my mind that I hear footsteps crack the snow behind us.

"Only a royal can be the next King," Aksel says as he approaches with Gier and Isak close behind. He throws the large sack he's carrying up over his shoulder effortlessly as his eagle eyes trace over me. He smiles and, frustratingly, it brightens his face. "I'm glad to see you out in the snow," he says. "You look like a Queen."

I straighten my back, hold my chin just a little higher. "I haven't passed all the trials yet."

Gier nods. "You will."

Isak's green eyes flash to him, then back to me. "Is everything to your liking so far?"

I nod. "Except the choice I have to make," I say, confidence rising from my core and out my throat. "Everything seems so... wonderful here. Except the hierarchy. Why are some more worthy than others?"

Aksel cocks his head. "That's what keeps things wonderful here, Anika."

"Annie," Soren corrects him quickly. He takes a single step closer.

Aksel's expression changes swiftly, a scowl taking the place of his once easy smile.

"It *is* just Annie," I say in his defense. "But just because something has always been a certain way doesn't mean it has to be like that always, right?"

Aksel's jaw tightens. His hard stare moves from Soren to me. "It does when magic is involved. You're just a girl–"

Soren takes another step closer to the three princes. His hand is outstretched as if he plans to hold me back. "She's a woman. A future Queen." His voice is a growl, his head tilted down just a little to catch Aksel's eyes. He's taller than the prince, but I can see it matters to him that he can really look at Aksel now, read his every minute expression.

I didn't mean to start anything. I feel almost bad I said anything, but I know I had to ask, had to speak my truth. Plus, it helps that Soren is here. He won't let anything hurt me, even my ego or my feelings, it seems.

I come forward now, right until I'm standing at Soren's outstretched hand. "I want to go home now," I say. I lean forward to get his attention and his intense eyes shift to me, softening every so slightly as they fall on my face.

Soren tilts his head to the three princes, an almost bow.

"Well," Vetle jumps in quickly, "Annie says she wants to go, so we go. We'll take you home." He nearly scoops my arm back into his, then turns us all away.

"It is your home," Aksel calls out to us as we make our way back down the hill. "And you'll learn the ways."

I bristle at his voice. At his warning.

At my suddenly tensed body, Vetle pulls me closer to him.

This is the fucking land of Santa Claus for fuck's sake. Can everyone just be more chill about hierarchies and politics for like one moment?

CHAPTER 15

Spirals

I t's when we're at the dimly lit lodge that Vetle's arm slips from mine. He smiles at me gently. "I'll go find you some food and your... running gear," he says as he opens the door for me.

Warm air embraces me as I walk through and there's a little tingle in my nose as I begin to heat up again after our long walk outside. I turn back to him but only smile. There's not much to say right now, but I appreciate that he's thought ahead to dinnertime for me.

He moves to the far door, runs his hand along it, and disappears from sight.

Soren enters behind me and the doors shut at last, blocking out the princes and the snow.

I flop onto the nearest couch, feet flinging into the air rather ungracefully. The pillows are plush and soft, the light here flickers gold and dim.

The elf sits on the other side of the couch slowly, as though I might attack him. He stares into the wall.

I roll over onto my back and prop a pillow beneath my head

so I can see him better. In the low light, the shadows across his face dace, accentuating the line of his strong jaw, the cut of his high cheekbones. He's sitting tall, straight, proper, with his hands holding each knee like a statue. His black hair shines in the low glow and I watch as his eyes narrow just a little when he notices that I'm studying him. "Thank you for standing up for me," I say at last.

His fingers clench but he turns to me. "It's my job," he says, his voice low.

"To watch out for me, yes," I say as I sit up on my elbows.

His eyes trail down me, then back up, lingering a little too long at my exposed collarbone.

My breath catches there, where his eyes follow the curve of my neck. "But..." I whisper, as though it's all I can get out. "But against your princes?"

His eyes find mine again. "Against anything that—"

"Seeks to harm me," I finish for him. "Right." I tear my eyes from his, leaning back against the pillow once more to stare at the high ceiling. I study the rafters. "Will the trials hurt me?"

"No," he says. "We wouldn't allow that."

I sigh. "I have a lot to learn about this place..." I think aloud. "Can you tell me what the next trial is?"

"I cannot," he says.

"Would that be breaking magical rules or something?"

"You have to discover your own magic yourself. Even if I told you what to expect and how to pass the last two trials, it wouldn't matter. It's all up to you. You get to choose."

I blink. "I still don't understand why."

A long silence descends over us and my mind races with the possibilities. There could be any number of reasons why. Or no reason at all. Maybe it's just random and I'm the lucky one out of billions. Maybe no one else was stupid enough to bring the weird elf doll into their house and keep it there overnight like some kind of petty thief.

In my defense, I did think they were cookies at first. Then a prank. Then I just didn't want the poor thing left out to the elements. When you think about it, I'm actually not at all to blame for any of this–

I groan and throw an arm over my face.

I feel a shift in the cushion next to me. Soren is leaning closer.

"I'm spiraling," I explain, though I keep my arm firmly over my eyes. I don't want to be any more embarrassed than I already am.

"You think you think too much?" His voice is low, but closer now.

I nod. "And not enough. Then I think too much about how I didn't think enough."

Soren hums, thoughtfully. The low vibration so close tickles my stomach.

"You have a spark," he says. "I want to help it grow."

"How?" I whisper. I move my arm a little, but all of the sudden, his hand is on me, holding my forearm over my eyes. My breath catches in my throat, a thrill runs from my arm down to my core.

"Can I show you?" he asks.

"Won't I need my eyes to see?"

He laughs, a low rumble and I flush instantly at the sound. I can see his smile in my mind, his damn cocky smile. "Oh no, I just want you to feel." His thumb traces down the inside of my wrist lightly.

I swallow. Hard.

"If that's alright with you."

"Yes," I breathe.

"Please?" he prompts.

How can someone so infuriating be so compelling? How can he make me feel like I'm on fire and secure all at once?

I nod.

"Say it."

My lips part. I take in a breath so my chest rises, stretching the fit of my dress, begging to be ripped off and set free. "Please," I whisper out.

"Beg."

The command has me tightening under his grip. I pull one leg up, making space for him between my thighs but he won't budge, won't move closer.

My lips tingle at the thought of his, so close and yet far enough to feel like an eternity. I bit the bottom lip to stop myself from trying to get closer to him. "Please," I say at last. "Please."

I want to stop thinking, just for a moment. I want to feel, come undone. I want to forget where I am, that any of this happened. I don't even know if I say any of this or if it's just desperate thoughts, all I know is that his hand on my wrist tightens and I feel the weight of him lower down my body, his free hand grazing lightly under my dress to the outside of my thigh.

I tremble, legs shaking with need. His touch is too light. Too slow.

"Please," I say again. "Soren, please."

His fingers suddenly press into my skin, pushing my legs further apart. "If you want me to stop," he says, "tell me. I will."

And I know it. The promise nests securely in my chest. I am

safe, even as his hand is still keeping me from any sight, even as he presses my dress up over my quivering thighs and I feel his breath, hot and deep against the inside of my knee. "Please... don't stop..."

His other hand traces the line of my leg, up to my already soaked core and his mouth follows.

Under any other circumstances, I'd be embarrassed that I'm not wearing any underwear. But right now? I'm just grateful it's one less thing in his way as my back arches up to meet his tongue that flicks just above my clit, warm and pulsing. I need this. I need him.

My hand goes to him, snaking through the soft feathers of his dark hair and I pull, trying to get him closer.

He tugs away. "Oh no," he scolds me, placing a row of light kisses along my other leg. "I tell you when."

Fuck. Everything out of his mouth is the sexiest thing I've ever heard. But I still can't help but buck my hips a little. "I need–"

"I know, Annie," he whispers. "Be patient."

"I can't." The words nearly cry out of me. My heart is slamming into my ribs. My ears ring a little. "Please, Soren. Please."

His grip on my arm tightens and needles run into my fingers. But I love it. I love all of it– the hard hold, the way his other arm wraps around my back, pulling me up to meet his mouth and *my god* his tongue plunging into me.

This time, I can't help the cry that escapes me, the whimper, loud and pitiful as he works his tongue into me, his lips rubbing the most sensitive part of me. His fingers press into my sides, holding me so still I could break.

And I do. I shatter into pieces as he finishes sucking at my clit until I unravel over again.

He lets go at last. Blood rushes back into my hand and my face. I keep my eyes shut for now, riding the aftershocks of my climax as it pulses through every inch of my body.

"Look at me," Soren orders.

My eyes flutter open, but everything is blurred.

Except him.

He's kneeled beside me now. His hand goes to my chin, gently guiding my face to really, truly, look at him.

"Anytime you find yourself spiraling," he murmurs. "You let me know."

I nod, leaning into his touch. My heart has only just begun to calm and here he is, holding me so carefully, threatening to have me back where we started. "Now...?" A smile flashes across my flushed cheeks.

Soren smiles back. He holds me firm as he places a ginger kiss on my forehead. "Not now."

"But I haven't... You didn't..."

"Don't worry about me." And that, too, sounds like an order. He lets go and rises in a steady, calm motion, only to lean back down as he effortlessly scoops me up into his arms like a bride.

I feel weightless. Effortless. Blissful. No worries here as I curl into his hold, nuzzle up against his hard chest and feel the gentle motion of his steps as he carries me to my bedroom.

V etle is back just as I get out of the shower. He has a tray in his hands and a flush on his cheeks as he watches me come out of the bathroom with just my white plush robe that doesn't extend past my knee.

I smile at him, still drying my hair with the towel.

Part of me feels a little guilty. Even though I don't know his true feelings, or if there are any at all, really. Still, the thought of his skin against mine makes me pause.

My eyes shift to Soren, who is sitting casually on the couch beside the bed. He looks at me with a half smile.

"Food's here," Vetle says. "Sorry it took me so long. I'm not used to working with chickpeas."

He sets the tray down and casts a glance at Soren. "It's good though, want me to make you a plate?"

Soren's smile grows, his eyes locked on mine. "No, I already ate."

OH MY GOD. I could die. I want to chase him from the room for that bad joke.

Still, Vetle doesn't seem to notice. He shrugs and pops a single roasted chickpea into his mouth from my plate and nods to himself as if confirming it really is good.

"Well, the next trial is ready," Vetle says. He slides the tray closer to me on the bed and gestures to it. "So eat up. It's almost time. You'll need your strength."

I let the little hair towel fall to the floor and hurry to the food, suddenly ravenous. "Is it more running?" I ask as I stuff a spoonful of the savory meal into my mouth. I groan as soon as the food hits my tongue. It's *delicious.* "Vetle, oh my god," I say with a full mouth.

Soren raises a brow at me, amused.

I flush and cover my mouth with one hand. "Sorry, but this is amazing."

Vetle stands taller. Honey hair falls into his eyes. "Well, thank you. It took more tries than I care to admit. Hence my tardiness."

I scoop more quickly. "Alright, can I get any clue about the next trial? Isn't it in your best interest that I pass? You know, for, like Christmas magic or whatever?"

"Nothing too strenuous, physically," Vetle says. He casts a long stare at Soren. "It'll be alright."

"She can handle it," he says simply.

And, somehow, despite how *incredibly ominous* that all sounded, I believe him.

CHAPTER 16

The Ghost of Christmas Present is a Little Tipsy

The same entourage of elves as before all stand before me. We're in a room that Vetle used magic to get to. One of those portal doors. And now, I'm stuck staring at a bunch of pointy-eared dudes who all look way too serious considering they're wearing what equates to fancy Santa suits.

The room is dark, and small, so they have to crowd each other just a little as I look at the snow globe in the center of the room, lit, it seems, from within. Honestly, the whole thing looks sinister as hell and part of me wonders if I stepped into a weird cult instead of the North Pole.

I raise a brow at the thing, then look at Gier. I know at least he won't give me the run around, though his diction will be a little more formal than I'd like. "What do I do... exactly?"

"Place your hand upon the glass dome and the trial will commence."

There it is. That damn language use. Does he think he's a King already? No one else talks like that. For whatever stupid reason, it bothers me.

Still, I walk up to the *glass dome*, and with one final look at Soren and Vetle, I 'place my hand upon' the top.

It's like I fell asleep. Except, I *fell* asleep. I feel like I've hit the floor and everything faded to black. So maybe it's more like I passed out...

When I recalibrate myself, I'm in the same room, except the elves are gone, replaced with a giant figure in a green, fur-lined robe that falls open to reveal his bare chest, and a holly wreath around his massive head. He smiles at me, jovial, almost drunk. "Welcome, future Queen," he says with his arms spread wide.

I squint at him. "Thanks..?"

"It's been 100 years since the last Queen, but I've been keeping busy," he goes on, either unconcerned or without noticing my hesitance and confusion.

"That's... nice," I say. I look around the room. Everything is the same. It's small, dimly lit. Am I supposed to escape? Fight this guy? I look down. I should have changed out of these damn dresses and into the freshly laundered running clothes. I mean, the elves literally washed them after purchasing. They could not have been more clear.

I ready my stance, though, I'm not sure where I'm off to.

The man raises a hand to stop me. "No, no, one of that," he says with a belly laugh. "The last Queen tried to offer me sweets. The one before that pulled a knife on me."

My posture softens. I stand taller, hands hanging at my sides limply. "Really?"

His laugh only grows, filling the room, *literally*, with light.

I look around as the light warms everything in sight with my mouth slightly open. "Okay," I say slowly, finding his face again. "So, what is the trial?"

"Come with me," he says, turning to the other side of the

room where a door with a large gold handle glimmers. He smiles back at me, then opens the door. "Your next trial is to be sure you want to be here. Follow me."

I do. I'm not sure if I'm compelled to, or if I just want it over with, but I follow him into the dark that lays beyond the door.

A *whoosh* of air blasts me in the face and I see my sister, her girlfriend, and their cats lounging in the living room of their apartment. A place I knew well, until I moved across the country.

"Krista!" I cry out, but she stays still, her back on the floor, one leg crossed over her knee, her foot bouncing in time to the music playing on her 'vintage' record player.

"They cannot hear or see you," the giant says as he comes close to me, his head bowed low so he doesn't hit the ceiling. He gestures at them, happy and warm and smiling. "I am here to show you what you are leaving behind."

My brows furrow. "But I thought–" I take a few steps closer to my sister, a dull ache already forming in my chest. "I thought I could still see her."

A laugh booms. So loud, I flinch, and eyes still on Krista, am shocked she didn't hear anything. "Of course you can," the man says. "As often as you would like. Except in winter."

I turn to him. "Like, all of winter?"

He nods, sadly. "From the Winter Solstice, to January 19."

My head shakes, I don't believe this. "So, literally three weeks?" I try to wrap my mind around those dates. Is there some kind of significance to them? Something I'm critically missing? I try to recall what they might mean, and then, my years reading my classmate's astrological charts comes to me. It was *a phase*, for sure, but fun. "Wait, like all of Capricorn season..?"

He nods.

"Seems arbitrary."

"It isn't," he assures me.

I frown. "But. I mean... it is."

His frown deepens. "I understand if it is too great a weight to hold," he says. He gestures at their tree with flickering lights, the little ornaments we had as kids, to the cookie jar on the counter, the one our great grandmother left us. "Will you be able to miss such memories?"

I deflate. But not with surrender. With pure relief. "Look." My hands find my hips. "Yeah, I think if I move to the North Pole, ironically, I'll see her more than my broke ass would when I have to save up to pay for flights." My stance changes as I shift to my other leg and watch my sister with a smile. "So I miss Christmases... I think I can handle that."

"Let me show you one more," he says with a wave of his hand and just like that, the same sudden *whooshing* sound invades my ears and we're in a home I don't recognize.

It's stark here. Undecorated, or at least, decorated with the least offensive items. Palatable crowd pleasing printed paintings of flowers hang on one white wall. There's a gray couch with dark green throw pillows that look as though they've never been touched.

"Where are we?" I turn to him.

"Do you know this place?" he asks.

My brows furrow and I try to place it but come up empty. "No..." I say. "Should I?"

He looks around, bending his massive head to see better as

he scans the room. "Oh, shit," he grumbles to himself. "Wrong house."

I laugh, though my brows remain in an intense and unflattering crinkle. "What? You're the ghost of freaking Christmas and you got the wrong house?"

"It happens," he says with a shrug. "I do this every 100 years, and no offense, it was hard to track down people you're close with to tempt you out of the deal to become the next Queen."

I pinch the brim of my nose. "I see... This trial is to see if I want it. Like, *really* want it? If I'll miss people back home too much."

A sting pierces my heart, though I wish it didn't. It was hard to track down people I love, people who love me. And I wish I could say that's because I'm some kind of harned badass, but the truth is, that the reality of it is just terribly depressing in a way that's not even dramatic like Elisabet's plague story.

I was a shy, lonely kid, with a big sister who helped me through most of my life. We moved around a lot so I never got close with any friends, and when I could afford to, I moved even further just to try my hand at doing things on my own.

And that adventure was, at least so far, a spectacular failure.

It wasn't like I had some horror befall my family, or that we were hiding from the mob. We were just poor, moved around too much in an attempt to find the right place, and so while people had friends since childhood, or even high school, I did not. While people had long term boyfriends, I found it hard to stay with anyone too long because, inevitably, someone would annoy me too much over something small and I'd bail.

I look at him now as he eyes me with sympathy, not pity, in his expression. All I can do is smile back. "Listen," I hold out a reassuring hand to him. "I passed this one on my own terms. Was I hesitant about this whole thing at first? Sure. I mean... they're *elves*. But. Now, I think that maybe this is where I was always meant to be." I look around at what I now realize is clearly a model home. "Well, not *here*. But there."

I want to add "With them" but I stop myself. They are not on the table. For whatever reason. And even if they were... still. *They*, two of them? Not just... *him*.

"Let's go home," I say with a gentle pat of his arm. "But, do me a favor?"

The giant nods slowly, the holly wreath falling a little sideways over his curls.

"Can you pretend this wasn't as easy for me as it was?"

He cocks his head.

I look away. "It's just... I'm tired of the sympathy. When people get all weird after finding out that I never had lasting friends and that I don't know most of my family." I trail off, my gaze to the floor. "Can we just. Not?"

He nods again, this time, with that damn sad face that most people make when they hear my extremely boring backstory.

I do my best to smile through it, to avoid telling him that *this* is why I avoid talking about it. When there are so many people in my own neighborhood with things so much more impactful happening to them, *this*, this right here is what annoys me.

"You may just be our true Queen afterall," he says quietly, and just like that, in a single blink, I'm back in the strange room, surrounded by princes and elves, and... I find Vetle, smiling at me brightly. Soren in the corner, his eyes alight.

"She passed," the Ghost of Christmas Present's voice echoes through the room.

And, though there is a burst of cheers, there's also a nagging feeling in my stomach that something isn't quite right. What did he mean by 'the true Queen'? Are there doubts? And if so, who has them? *Or...* I wonder as the worry takes root in my chest, *Are all the other Queens placeholders?*

I shake the thought from my mind. What in the 'chosen one' B.S. have I been riding on to think that I am not just special but the specialist of the specials? I need to knock that off before my head gets too big.

Aksel catches my eye and a chill runs down my spine under his intense stare. It's as though he's read my thoughts. He has a way of looking not just at me but... into me.

I pry my eyes away just as a surge of heat rushes through me and into my fingertips.

The Armored Dress

I'm starving.

I have no idea what this surge of magic was, but it was enough to make me ravenous.

As I wander the halls, looking again for that kitchen to forage, I hear footsteps close behind, hurrying to catch up.

"You did it!" Vetle says, joyously. "I'm proud of you. I mean, I knew you could do it, of course. But I have heard that the second challenge is the hardest."

I sigh, but keep moving, avoiding his face, perfectly symmetrical and adorably happy, at all costs. "It was..." I say, carefully, "very difficult, but I managed. It's only a few weeks of the year that I can't travel." At last, I look up at him as we walk. "Are Capricorns special or something? Why *can't* I travel to see my family and, um, friends, during that time?"

Vetle waves a hand. "Rules beyond my scope," he says. "Perhaps when you are Queen, you will change them?" He looks at me with a soft expression. "Where are you off to in such a hurry?"

"Kitchen. I'm hungry."

He skips ahead of me a few steps. "Follow me, my Queen."

Vetle's hands are skilled. It's like watching a trained chef at work. Fire and salt and brightly colored vegetables fling through the air with precision and art. It's masterful to watch, and, as a bead of sweat buds at his brow, also... delicious.

I pull my eyes away, focusing instead on the glow of the stainless steel counter. I shift on the stool until my chin rests in my hand. I could get used to this– the thoughtfully prepared meals made by someone who cares. Watching him work, with his sleeves rolled up, knowing he'll keep me safe...

A blush betrays me and I grip the counter, hard. Before I can stop myself, I ask the question that's been lingering under the surface since our time in bed together. "Are you really happy?"

Vetle continues to saute, a little burst of fire forms at the star pointed stove as he shifts the skillet with one hand. "Of course."

"With the hierarchy here, too?" I prompt further. I've already said so much, I may as well just ask what's truly on my mind.

Vetle's eyes shift to me, for just a fleeting second, then he's back, focused and thorough at the stove. "Why?"

I pull back, sitting up straighter. "You always seem so happy," I say at last. "I just..." *wonder if it's all a facade. Like I used to have to pretend.*

Vetle clicks the gas stove off. He plates my dish on a cream ceramic and slides it across for me, still steaming and smelling of fragrant species and oil. His smile widens. "I like to be of service," he says with a small bow, as if to truly drive home the point. As if from magic, he produces a fork and sharp knife for me and hands them over with his classic golden retriever smile. "Eat up. You need it."

I do. And, like always, it's one of the best meals I've ever had.

I'm satiated, at least... in a sense. But the look the giant gave me in the second trial, and the fact that one of the hardest parts of becoming Queen, the part where you say goodbye to loved ones during the holidays, was easy to me, just... stings. It leaves an emptiness in me that no amount of amazingly delicious home cooked meals can fill.

It sucks. And that's all there is to it.

We reach my door and Vetle gives me a quick nod before taking a few steps back.

My hand lingers on the handle and I turn to him. "Come in?" I ask, my voice almost hoarse.

Vetle's face softens. He nods, and slips in behind me.

I close the door with a definitive *click*. As soon as it's shut, though, I feel the weight of everything on me.

I cross the dimly lit room to my bed and stare at it for a long moment.

It's not until Vetle speaks that I break my thoughts.

"I am happy," he says quietly. "But I wish..."

Turning to him, I catch the hint of pain across his face before he is able to look down at the floor. There's the familiar look of a pain inside him that I cannot reach. Not yet.

I close the space between us and, when I'm near, my hand finds his chin. I cup it gently, so careful as though he may break under my grip. But instead, he leans in, one hand rising to envelope mine, holding it close to his cheek as he shutters a sigh.

"I missed your touch," he whispers in my hand, his lips fluttering along my palm, sending sparks flying through my arm and down deep within me.

Before I can think, I press up onto my toes and my hand snakes around his thick neck to pull him down to me. Our lips collide and his mouth parts easily for me as my tongue slides into his warm mouth.

He shudders. His whole body melts at my touch and he folds around me, arms encircling my waist and upper back until I'm pressed against his chest and heat flares into me.

I want to take care of him. I want to destroy him. I want to rebuild him.

I pull my mouth from his, and his eyes darken. His quick, heavy breaths come out ragged as he scans my face for signs of what I mean by breaking us apart.

"Go to the bed," I say with a light push against his chest.

Immediately, his arms fall. He looks to me, then to the bed, but does as he's told.

"Am I your Queen?" I ask, crossing the room with slow, steady steps. I want this. More than anything, I want this. But I need to know if he does too. Or if he is simply commanded to. I can't stand the thought of taking advantage.

He nods. Swallows. His fingers twitch at his sides.

"I don't want to be," I whisper. "Not now. I just want to be me."

He nods again, understanding. "I can't get you out of my mind, Annie," he says, stepping closer to close the gap between us again. "I'll do as you command. Not as my Queen. Not as your guard. As you are. As I am."

I smile. Relief. Power. Magic. It all fills me up but the ache between my legs is still begging to be filled. "Strip," I say, my voice so authoritative that I surprise myself.

He does, carefully, and standing before me is the most impressive statue of a man I have ever seen. Every inch of him is absolute perfection, sculpted from steel and sunlight. Tight muscles tense under my stare as I look him over until I reach his hard, throbbing cock, already leaking a glistening bead for me.

My hands graze over his chest and everywhere I go, raised goosebumps follow. "Do you want this?" I ask one final time.

"Yes. Annie." His words come out slowly and I can sense the lump in his throat. The feeling of needing, desperately, but not knowing how...

"Lay back," I command, pushing his chest just a little so he knows I'm serious.

He falls back on the plush bed, propped on his elbows, and staring at me with hunger in his honey eyes. Between his legs, his desire is clear, and, as I climb onto the bed, realize it's one of the biggest I've ever seen.

"I said, 'lay back'," I say again as my hands find his corded thighs.

He shivers at my touch but does as I ask, his head falls back onto the thick pillows behind him. He lets out a small groan as my hands work their way up his muscled legs and to his lower abdomen, teasing every inch except what I know he wants most.

I watch him, a smirk falling on my lips as his eyes close and his brows knit in desperate need. Another moan escapes his lips as my fingers lightly brush against his most sensitive part, it moves at my touch, begging for more.

Looking down now at him, my fingers run up his impressive length, and my thumb grazes the tip just enough to elicit another needy sigh from him. It's addicting. But I can't keep this up for long either. Already, I find my mouth wanting.

His hands find my arms and he gently strokes me, from my hands up to my shoulders.

I shrug him off. "Do you want me to touch you?" I ask.

He nods. "Annie, yes."

My smile widens. "Then you can't touch me."

His eyes fly open just as my mouth finds his tip. I open wide to take as much of him in as I can. I open my throat for more, and I'm less than halfway.

A deep rumble shakes me and his hands grip at the blankets, long fingers finding their way into the layers quickly. His legs tremble beneath me as slowly I try to force myself lower, both hands working him as I do.

I can feel myself getting wetter at his sounds, the catching of his breath, as I rise up and my tongue flicks at his tip. The dark moans driving me wild as I lower quickly, hands and mouth working in unison. His hips buck at me and I know he won't last long like this.

Part of me, the darkest part, wants to let go. To edge him until he begs me to finish him. But I don't stop now. I keep my steady pace, tongue wrapping around him as I work my head up and down, faster now.

"I'm close..." Vetle's voice shakes. His back arches into me, one leg moves up as I straddle it, and I press down on his thigh with my body, feeling the ache between my legs instantly eased at the pressure of his leg on my clit. He starts again, "Do you...?"

I hum in response.

Consent.

Hunger.

Need.

I suck at his length as hard as I can and push down, opening my throat to fit as much of him as possible.

He cries out, hands fly up, grasping my hair in fists as he holds my head in place and my eyes sting as my jaw loosens and I swallow again and again and again.

Red is for Christmas

I don't know why what I just did feels both so wrong... and so perfect.

As I lay in bed, alone and yet fulfilled, I can't help but think about what my future here will bring. I have to choose one of the princes. Right? But so far, none of them have made me feel full of light the way *they* do. I don't feel *safe* with the princes like I do when I'm at Soren's side, or in Vetle's arms. They don't feed me. Make me laugh. Hell, I don't feel powerful with them. But worst of all, I don't feel... anything.

But I am to be a Queen, aren't I? I'm supposed to be the one to lead, to guide, to... *Fuck.* I don't even know. *Make Christmas magic happen?*

And all I can think of is that just outside my door, there's two elves. Two very different, very sexy, elves. And I'm doing my best but also failing at not falling for them.

I burrow lower in my covers and imagine what it might be like to not have to choose, to feel Soren's strong grip on my thighs, pulling me closer, and Vetle's huge cock slide into me, filling me up completely. I shiver at the thought and find my mouth aching for more, my walls flutter around my fingers as I palm myself into a quiet and quick release.

It's early morning when I wake, rested but an unease grips my chest.

I turn over in the bed and breathe in deeply. Vetle's scent, cinnamon and fresh spice, lingers on my pillow. I pull the pillow closer and take another long breath, savoring the memories of last night.

It's short lived, however.

Cat's voice echoes in my mind as if she's speaking to me through a distant microphone, "Can I come in?"

I groan, rolling back over onto my back. "Yes," I say aloud and her face appears through the door, followed quickly by the rest of her body as she slinks in, her fluffy fur moving with her like puffy clouds.

"The princes have prepared you a breakfast," she says, casually as she stalks up to the foot of the bed. "I think someone scolded them for not spending time with you."

Who? I want to ask so I can tell them to butt out of it. I don't particularly want to spend time with them. I want to pass the trials and worry about the choice later. But I keep the question to myself.

Because it doesn't matter who. I know just as well that I *do* need to pick one of them and for whatever reason, they all seem to be waiting for me to really prove myself before making any effort. That is, except for Aksel. Who, really, I would rather he make *less* effort to be near me.

Sure, he's good looking. Tall and lean with the face of a

Hallmark protagonist. But he's also a jerk and seems quite content to benefit from his status while putting others down.

Which just seems excessive. He's already a prince. Does he really need to also prove it by throwing his weight around?

Maybe Isak, quiet and fierce looking, is the better option.

I fall back into my pillow again. "Do I have to go?"

Cat walks the perimeter of my room. "Vetle told me to tell you he's the chef, if that helps."

It does.

And doesn't.

Cat's stare falls on me at last. "And he wanted you to know that he put Soren in charge of the hot chocolate."

My eyes widen.

That *is* good to know. I kind of hope the princes have to drink it to avoid seeming impolite. At the very least, it would be funny to watch.

"Where is Vetle?"

"Getting the finishing touches on the dishes."

"And Soren? Aren't I supposed to be guarded at all times?"

Cat looks like I've asked her something offensive. But, that's just kind of a cat's way, even if the cat is a giant, magic one. "I am escorting you. I can protect you plenty, trust me."

"And keep me from escaping?"

Cat's eyes narrow. "You want to escape?"

I laugh. "No, not all. I just still don't really understand why I have bodyguards at all. If it's for my sake or," I gesture broadly, "theirs."

Cat lets out a little huff. "There are things here that can... sneak up on you, until you're officially Queen."

"Sinister," I grumble.

Cat either didn't hear me, or chose not to comment. She

flicks her massive tail and says, "Come on, get yourself all dressed. I suggest one of the red dresses."

I raise a brow. "Why red?"

"Seems like your color," is all Cat says before disappearing again.

In the large wooden chest, I find my new running clothes. Black leggings, running shoes, about four different pairs, actually, and a variety of zip up athletic tops. I pull the pink up and study it. If I was being real with myself, this is what I'd wear every day here.

But, I guess I can suck it up for a few events.

Like breakfast.

With men I have only passing interest in but am supposed to *literally magically* fall madly in love with after the last trial.

It's a lot of pressure, and I decide to let Cat's advice take one thing off my plate. Just one decision made for me helps when I have a million things swirling in my mind. I pull out the red dress, heavy and well constructed, with long tight sleeves and golden threads woven in leaf patterns along the hems and over the plunging bust.

It's formal for breakfast, but what the hell? I'm a queen, after all.

Almost.

I pull it on over my body and find it fitting everywhere perfectly. Despite the heavy material, it's softly hugging my waist and hips until it flares out to graze the floor. I lift my arms and do a little spin, letting it dance around me like flower petals. I stare down at the dress, the way the neckline clings to my collarbone with a deep v, exposing the hint of my breasts beneath.

Just enough to be tempting, I think.

It feels amazing.

I hurry to the bathroom to fix up my hair into a low braid and wash off my face. *I can do this,* I think as I give myself a quick glance in the mirror. *Use the dress like armor.*

C at escorts me down the hall and through the portal door to the dining room. The large window overlooks a wintery scene where pink and blue in the sky reflect off the crystalized earth. It lets in just enough gentle, cold morning light to contrast the warm glow of the fires inside.

The long table is laid out with candles and a variety of dishes, all, thankfully, vegetarian, it seems. My chest expands, and I find myself smiling at the elaborate spread.

It only grows when I catch Vetle's eyes in the corner of the room. He holds his hands out to the table as if to ask if I like it.

My gaze shifts to Soren in the other corner, half in shadow of the flickering candle light. He gives me a knowing look, like he's trying to tell me something, but I can't decipher it.

"Happy picking," Cat says slyly as she disappears.

Damn. I almost forgot why I'm actually here. The princes sit at the far end of the table, rising slowly now that I am here. I try my best to look at them. To truly see them now in the morning glow mixed with dancing warm light.

Aksel, the tallest and leanest of them, gives a quick bow of his head and the others follow his lead. So he is the leader, then. At least, to some degree. I had figured that much, but if there was any doubt about who's calling the shots here, it's gone now.

Still, Geir appears to be the oldest, though it's hard to say if that's true or if his stern expression simply ages him. His jaw is set tight, posture stiff, he looks ready to spring at any moment.

He doesn't smile at me, and honestly, I can't imagine ever seeing his expression change from anything other than either boredom or discomfort.

Isak, meanwhile, with his green gaze, hands in his pockets, and a wolfish grin unnerves me. He's attractive, objectively. But he's got that certain something that if I met him on a date, I'd probably keep my phone in my lap, ready to make a quick escape. Call it gut instinct, or my brain picking up on something small that my consciousness isn't aware of. With him, it's like some body movement that looks off, or the way he watches me, there's just something I can't shake that I just don't like.

The moment passes quickly, though, and Geir motions for me to join them at the table.

I approach slowly, my eyes shifting from Soren to Vetle as Askel pulls out the chair at the head of the table so my back is to my guards.

I sit, stiffly, looking at each prince again in turn. "Thank you for the breakfast," I say at last, mostly to Vetle, though I don't know if he hears me.

Aksel smiles and raises a glass in a type of cheers.

"Of course," Isak says, a bit too chipper for my liking. "We have all been so busy with everything, we neglected to make time for you, the reason we are all here."

"Our apologies, my Queen," Geir adds with a slow nod.

I do my best to smile. "Thanks," I say as I lean forward a little to look at the food laid out before us. I point to an omelet that appears to be stuffed full of peppers and mushrooms. "Do you mind if I start?"

Aksel snaps his fingers, a loud click that startles me. "Your Queen has asked for..." he leans in to inspect it. "What is this?"

"An omelet," Vetle says as he hurries over to me. He slices a quarter of it and places it gently on the plate in front of me.

I look up at him, his face is close to mine, heat flashes through me for the moment, then he's back to the corner. "I can get it myself," I say, my voice comes out a bit harsher than I meant it to as my body twists to catch his eyes, then to Soren. I move back to face Aksel with what I hope looks like determination and not desperation. "Are they not joining us?"

Aksel scoffs as if I just asked if he thinks gravity is real. "You are royalty now," he says. His eyes rake down my body, examining the top of my brow to the rise and fall of my chest. "What made you pick this color today?"

I look at each of them, realizing now that I've only seen Aksel in black, besides his silly Santa hat that first night. Isak has always been wearing a dark shade of green to match his eyes. And Geir has always been in deep blue.

Are they on some kind of team or something?

I can feel Vetle and Soren's eyes on me, waiting for what I'll say next. I look down at my dress. It's the same shade of red that they wear... "I like red," I say at last. "It suits me."

Aksel's face hardens.

"Is it not what Santa wears, traditionally?" I try to diffuse some nerves I seem to have struck, though part of me wants to keep stoking the fire, to see how far I can push him to break his facade of being 'kingly'.

Aksel leans back in his chair, a half smile on his lips. "Of course," he says and his smile grows. "You look stunning."

"Radiant," Isak adds.

"Regal," Geir agrees.

I shake my head, poke the omelet with my gold fork. "I'm

not royal yet," I say at last. The fork clanks onto the plate as I drop it. "I think they should join us."

Geir leans forward, his hand over his cup like he's defending it. "You are not queen yet. So we will make the rules."

My fingers curl in my lap. "Then I'll take my food to go," I say through clenched teeth.

Aksel waves his hand, as if dispelling the tension from the air. "My Queen," he says and I cringe at the *my* in his phrase. "Let me tell you a little about our world. We are the princes of Christmas. Chosen not by birth but experience, with trials of our own, the likes of which you cannot begin to imagine. We *earned* our position here. We earned the right to have you choose one of us and provide you a life of magic and happiness." His hand rests on the table now, palm up. He looks at me as though he expects me to take it.

I keep my hard stare on his eyes. How can he possibly know what I am able to imagine? How can he not understand that fighting for the right to be king doesn't mean you get to be a dick to everyone else?

He goes on, "You will be happy here. If you let yourself be. You passed the second trial, the one that determines if you want it enough to stay. And do you not feel your magic grow?"

I look away, heat rising to my ears. I do. I feel it grow with each passing moment. But... I don't think it's all the trials. It can't be.

I'm actually *truly* finding myself here. My confidence and my weakness. It's not something that's being bestowed upon me. It's something that I, too, am earning.

"Your time here has been short, but understand the reality of it," he says. "Without a King, there is no Christmas. Without a Queen, it all falls apart. You will need to learn to fit in here."

Tears sting at the corners of my eyes before I can keep them at bay. Fitting in. I've never been good about that no matter how hard I try. I rise up from my seat, this was a mistake.

All of it.

"She is our Queen," Soren's voice, low and stern, rises with me. He is at my side in a blink. He is not touching me, but his closeness lends me support though I cannot truly lean on him. "You will not tell her how to conduct herself."

"And you, guard, will not speak to us like this."

The princes all stand as one, their bodies angled forward as if ready to strike.

Cat materializes at my other side. She hisses, a loud snake-like sound cutting through the air. "Enough of this," she says, her usual high pitch voice gone, replaced instead by a low snarl. "You are making fools of yourselves." She eyes each prince, then me.

I'm included in the foolishness? What the hell?

"The next trial should be ready by this evening. You all need to be ready." She looks down at my plate. "So, yes, take the food to go."

"I'll get it," Vetle says, quickly and a little too brightly.

He's probably just as eager to get out here as I am.

Leaning over me, he scoops up my plate and adds extra helpings of potatoes and fruit. He steals a glance at me quickly before handing me the food.

"Thank you," I whisper. To him. To Soren. Hell, to Cat.

And so, with the three of them close behind, we leave the princes to the rest of the breakfast with their own miserable company.

CHAPTER 19

Catching a Gingerbread Man is Actually Very Easy

Guilt nags at my stomach. Or... maybe it's hunger. I haven't actually eaten much of my breakfast. I'm too anxious to try.

Vetle looks a little glum about it. Which seems fair. He must have worked hard to prepare it all. His eyes keep shifting from me, to the plate, then back again.

Meanwhile, Soren has stood with his back to the closed door, arms crossed, looking pissed since we got in here. I'm not sure what to make of his expression except maybe he feels he went too far with the princes.

I poke at my plate a little more, picking out the green bell peppers mostly for something to do.

Cat is long gone after a gentle scolding to all of us about our poor behavior. To which, at least, Soren argued had nothing to do with Vetle. And it's true. Poor elf was just standing there hoping we'd eat food he clearly spent a lot of time preparing.

I stuff a few large bites into my mouth and he beams.

"What's their deal anyway?" I cover my mouth with one

hand and speak though I'm still chewing. Not lady-like, as my mother would point out if she was here.

Soren raises a brow, his posture softens a little. "They think they already run the place, don't worry about them."

"Were they always like that?"

Vetle and Soren exchange lingering looks.

"Yes, pretty much," Vetle says at last. He sighs, then indicates for me to take another bite.

I do, slowly.

"Are you ready?" Vetle says to Soren, his tone is quiet and gentle.

Soren nods, just the faintest tip of his head forward. His eyes are on me, cutting into my core.

I furrow. "For what?"

Vetle's smile is kind. "The last trial. Do you feel ready?"

"I've heard the second one is the hardest," I say, confidence filling my voice.

Other than a brief moment where I almost *technically* died, the trials have been easy. I'm not worried. With every passing trial, and every moment alone with *them*, I can feel myself becoming.

Becoming who I was meant to be.

Not the awkward kid.

Or the teen with no friends.

Not the adult with a dead-end job, a dusty vision board of unfulfilled dreams, and empty wrapped boxes under cheap second hand trees.

"I got this," I confirm again and finish my plate.

"I have no doubt," Soren says and slips out of the room.

"We'll be back," Vetle says and follows him.

Before the door shuts, I lunge forward. "Wait!"

He stops, hand on the door.

"Can I go explore the village? Or go for a run..?"

He shakes his head sadly. "I'm sorry, the trial is coming. You'll need your rest. And we need to accompany you."

I sigh, hands fall to my sides in defeat.

"Soren brought you books," he says as a consolation, pointing to the chest. "Things he thought you'd enjoy."

I cast a look to the chest, and the door clicks shut.

I'm not sure how Soren knows what I like to read, but I find myself going to the chest anyway. There's not much else to do and I'll take anything at this point.

I pull out the books slowly, and am surprised to find that they are all, in fact, absolutely my favorites. A series on a cozy, humorous detective agency. A trilogy with a talking cat and a ghost. Another series of what appear to be *very* spicy magicians that I haven't read yet but has been on my wishlist for a long time.

The door is still shut, and I doubt that he's still waiting outside. But I have to admit, he does know exactly what I like to read. I turn over one of the books in my hand, one that's been on my TBR for forever but I never go around to.

Did he stalk my Goodreads? I nearly laugh at the thought of Soren, elf warrior, scrolling through social media to find what I enjoy. Or, I wonder, maybe he just gets me more than he lets on. He is always watching, listening, and despite his calm demeanor, he seems to catch more than any of us realize.

Afterall, he *definitely* understood my body and my mind well enough the other day...

I clear the thought from my mind.

It's time to focus.

On magical smut.

. . .

I'm awoken with the startling realization that I fell asleep mid chapter, just as the two leads were finally having a moment... and then, the darker realization that I am not in my own bed.

It's not cold. Not really.

But I'm laying on a hard stone floor in a mostly darkened room and I've got a terrible soreness in my neck that comes from a night of sleeping with a bad hotel pillow.

How long have I been laying here?

I push myself up, dust my hands off on my leggings, grateful that I changed into my comfy athletic clothes before I curled up with my magician smut.

Looking around, the place looks very much like a dungeon. It's probably the best way to describe my situation. Gray stone floors, one torchlight on a sconce at the far wall, and a single, very worn wooden door beside it.

The passing consideration that maybe I *really* offended Aksel and I've been thrown into the opposite of a Santa workshop crosses my mind.

They wouldn't.

Right?

I squint into the dark, completely unsure about what I'm supposed to be doing. Do I go through the door? Wait to be rescued? Just scream my head off that I demand to be treated like a queen?

Seems unlikely, but maybe it is a test of character and they're waiting to see if I've got the Queen-like attitude.

Before I can overthink it any further, I force myself to walk toward the door, listening softly with my ear to the weathered wood. I wait there for a few moments but I can't hear anything.

Slowly, the door creaks as I open it.

Peeking through the crack, I'm met with a sight I never could have anticipated.

I was not in a dungeon after all, but rather some kind of closet, tucked into the corner of a massive library.

My mouth falls open as I slip through the door. It's dark here, a domed glass roof lets in some diluted aurora light, raining down over the several stories of shelves and old spined books. Ladders perch along some of the shelves, and for a moment, all I want to do is hop on one, slide it across the books with my hand running along their delicate spines while singing that I just want more than this provincial life.

Of course, I am a terrible singer and they'd all probably call the trial a wash right then and there.

So instead, I venture out into the shadows slowly, my eyes darting from shelf to shelf, and up a large staircase that leads up to the open floor above where even more books await.

Am I supposed to locate a special book of Christmas spells? Find my way out? Discover the *perfect* book?

But then, a blur from the corner of my vision catches my attention.

I spin toward it, muscles in my legs already tightening. I should have asked Cat for mace. I used to carry it on every run.

And I asked for headphones instead.

Stupid.

"Hello?" I call weakly.

For every other trial, I had been around the elves, I was ready-ish, and they wished me luck. This time, I've been kidnapped from my bed, deposited in a library with a freaky thing in here.

Seems brutally unfair to change the rules at the last trial.

I snag another glimpse of something from the other side and turn. My heart slams into my chest, beating rapidly beneath my running jacket. My fingers clench and I move so my back is to one of the giant bookshelves.

The light of the aurora overhead gives the space in the dark a dream-like quality, as though I'm actually underwater and shimmering light casts down from the surface and deep into the bottom floor.

But though it would be gorgeous under any other circumstances, I can't help the terror that seeps into every fiber of my being. I'm trapped here, with something waiting in the dark.

My back safely against the wood of the shelves, I call out again, "Hello? Hi, um. My name is Annie... I'm supposed to be doing the final Chestnut trial." I look into the shadows, eyes searching for any movement. "Which sounds crazy," I murmur to myself.

I lean forward, voice louder again. "Can you come out of the shadows? This is freaking me out and honestly, everyone here has been really nice so far so I doubt you mean any harm." I pause, then quieter say, "Okay, that is a lie. Some elves are kind of jerks, but still."

Soren promised no harm would befall me. At every turn, he stood up for me. Even against royalty. Even, weirdly, against myself.

I take a deep breath, steadying my raging heart.

From the shadows, a form emerges. It's human, or human-like. Tall, broad, heavy limbs and a shockingly large head. It lumbers forward toward me with a strange movement.

The way it's advancing, though, makes me pause.

It seems as hesitant as I am.

Pushing off the shelf with one hand, I keep my eyes focused on the figure ahead until, at last, it comes into the dim light.

I stifle a scream, hands clasp up over my mouth as I see before me a massive, living gingerbread man.

I feel like the creature and I have walked into a Shrek movie. It has to be a costume, or they gave me some kind of wild psychedelic before dropping me off in here.

But the way it moves looks so real. I can see the details of the crystal sugar on its gumdrop buttons, the cookie texture of its body. I gaze into its icing eyes, and see, strangely, life there.

My hands lower slowly, and I approach it with caution. "Can you speak?" I ask, then cringe. I'm not sure if it's offensive or not. It feels wrong, talking to a gingerbread cookie the size of a person. It feels even worse that it looks pained.

The gingerbread raises a handless arm and shakes its head 'no'.

I nod back, taking a few more steps closer.

It withdraws from me, retreating back into the darkness a little.

"Please don't," I call out, one hand reaching out to it. "I'm not afraid."

The gingerbread comes back into the light, slowly.

"It's okay," I tell it. I move my body lower until I'm sitting down under the shimmering light. "Can you sit with me?"

The gingerbread does, totally ungracefully and I feel a little bad asking it to do so when it clearly has trouble with complicated movements. Still, as we stare at each other. With its black icing eyes seeming to search my face, it leans forward just a little.

"Is this part of the last trial?" I ask, cringing at the selfishness of the question. Still, there's something about this creature that makes me think there's more than meets the eye.

The gingerbread nods, just once.

My eyes dart around its face, searching for more clues as to what I'm supposed to do, what I'm supposed to say. I wait, counting the beats of my aching heart trapped in my chest. Why am I so sure the creature is pained..? I decide to ask, point blank. "Are you hurting?"

It nods, again, just the little tilt of its head.

I lean forward, my hands resting on the cold stone floor so I can come closer. But for every inch I move forward, it pulls back. It doesn't want me to see it, not too closely.

Why?

And why here?

On all fours now, I am close to the sitting creature and it can no longer move any further from me unless it gets up and runs. I watch its eyes, waiting for a clue until, at last, it moves its body up toward me, towering over me.

I take in one shaking breath, then reach a hand up to its face.

It flinches but does not withdraw.

"If I were to tell you that I needed something..." I look away for a moment, unsure of how to phrase the next part, but then, my eyes are drawn back to it. I hold its gaze and my thumb traces the edge of its face. "If I needed you, in any capacity, would you be there?"

The head tilts again. Just a little.

My heart hits my chest like it is about to break away from me. "What happened to you..? Soren." His name chokes out of my throat, my eyes already filled with stinging tears.

A puff of white, hot smoke fills the space. My hair flies back, arms over my face to shield me from the heat and the intensity of it. Everything aches, though I don't know if it is from the smoke or the realization that Soren is hurting, turned against his will into... a cookie.

The smoke dissipates, and Soren, the Soren I know, sits among the smoldering steam, his head hung low, body wrapped tightly into himself.

"Soren!" I fling myself around him, though it's little use. I don't know what kind of protection my frame can provide, but I want to give it. My fingers dig into his skin, pulling him as tightly into myself as I can.

It is only then that I realize... I'm touching skin. Soren is completely, utterly, naked.

My face burns as I finally release him from my grasp. I pull away just enough to catch his eyes, tilt his face toward me with both hands. "Are you alright?" I breathe out the words in relief as his familiar, intense eyes meet mine, as I feel the spark of his skin against mine.

A half smile quirks up, though his brows furrow with a hint of pain. "You passed the last trial," he says quietly. "You caught the gingerbread man."

I look around the empty library, expecting the familiar fan fare of every other time before, but it's quiet still. I sink before him.

"No one will be here until dawn," he explains, his voice a little hoarse.

I pull him back into a tight embrace before I have the chance to think.

CHAPTER 20

A Darker Kind of Magic

We spend the night in each other's arms. And though nothing happens between us, he wraps his body around me as if still trying to keep me safe. *Me.* After everything he went through. I mean, he turned into a fucking gingerbread. I had no idea *that* kind of magic was possible.

I hate everything about it.

He hasn't said much, his usual domineering attitude is gone, replaced with something fragile. I never want to let him go. At least, not until he comes back to me, fully.

I run my fingers through his hair and he pulls me closer, head nuzzled into my chest and breathing deeply as if trying to take me all in.

It's not quite dawn when he finally speaks, jolting me from my half sleep.

"Every final test is different," he says. "But it always involves a darker kind of magic."

I look down, and he moves, fully extending to encase himself around me like a warm cocoon. I'm not sure if it's because he can now, that his strength has fully returned, or if it's because he doesn't want me to see his face now.

Either way, I wrap my arm around his back, tracing the lines of tightly coiled muscle and pull myself deeper into his embrace. "Did you know? That this is what they would do to you?"

I feel his nod, the small tilt of his head, against the top of mine.

"Why did you still go?"

He breathes in deeply, my whole body moves as his chest expands. "You deserve to have your magic," he says. "And the puzzle was simple. I'd know you anywhere, by your racing mind, or your light footsteps. By the smell of you in a crowded room, or by the laugh you don't give so easily." His voice is dark, it vibrates against my body, coiling me into tight spirals. "I knew you would know me too."

I squeeze my eyes shut, breathe him in. "How do you know me?" I ask the dreaded question, the one I've been afraid of. "How do I know you?"

Soren laughs, a deep, rumbling sound that sends a shock-wave through me. I could listen to that sound all night. It's genuine, and honest... and fucking hot. "Magic," he says simply.

"But I don't understa–"

Before I can complete the word, his lips are on mine, over-taking me with a desperation that clears my mind. My thoughts are a dark and turbulent sea, and his lips are oxygen. There's nothing else that matters now, just the feeling of electricity between us, of the burning need that floods through me.

Soren breaks away, and in a swift motion, pins my hands up over my head to the hard floor. My wrists are captured in his one large hand while the other works the zipper off my jacket. "I can show you," he growls in my ear.

"Yes," I breathe back, arching my back to get closer to him.

He laughs again. It rings through my ears like bright bells. He knows he has me... and I want him all the more for it.

He lets go of me, almost pushing my hands free from his aching grip. "Stand up," he says.

I'm not sure I even can. I scramble to my feet with shaking legs.

"Undress for me."

Clothes fall to the floor faster than I thought possible. I stand before him, completely as I am. Just enough chill to the air that my nipples point, desperate for touch. I can already feel the heat pooling in my lower abdomen.

And, because it's him, with his intense eyes, the time he takes to look at me completely, I feel more seen than I ever have. And yet... I don't feel self conscious. I feel like a Queen, standing before a god.

"On your knees," he says as he rises up, standing in front of me. The size of him, every inch of his body muscled and hard, sends a shiver up my spine though my skin is on fire.

I drop to my knees, hitting the floor hard. A blooming pain blossoms there and I. Love. It. It's just enough to clear my thoughts.

Nothing else matters right now. Just him and me and his words.

Soren steps closer, and my eyes widen at his impressive length. He smiles down at me and I nearly crumble. My mouth opens, and I feel so entirely empty.

He grabs a fistful of my hair, hard, lifting me so my eyes are back on his. Still, as I find his stare, his fingers loosen, the tips of them rub a small circle into my scalp. "Tell me you want me," he says.

"More than anything."

More than air.

More than magic.

More than being chosen by a prince.

His lips turn up. "Good."

I lean in but he tugs me away.

"You're going to tap twice if it's too much," he says, his voice deadly serious.

I nod.

"Say it."

"Tap twice... If it's too much."

He smirks, then pulls my head toward him.

I open wide as the tip of his throbbing cock pushes into my mouth.

"That's it, Annie," he groans, so low I'm not sure I heard him. He pushes further and I choke. "You can take it."

It's... huge. I try to open my throat as more of him breaks through the back of my mouth. Hands fly up to him and I try to work him slower the way I did with Vetle, but it's no use.

"Let go," he says and his fingers dig stronger into my hair.

I do but without my permission, tears begin to form in my eyes. I breathe in deep through my nose, inhale the scent of him as I do. It calms me, just a little. And excites me all the same.

"Put your hands behind your back," he says.

My eyes flick up to him but his face is serious. I do as I'm told, lacing my fingers behind me quickly.

He pushes in deeper and I gag, spit forming in the back of my throat. Still, my tongue wraps around him, I suck as hard as I can. I feel incredible. I feel infinite. The sounds he's making are all for me. All because of me.

His hold on me tightens. "Damn it, Annie," he moans as he

pulls out, just enough for me to breathe, to relax my jaw for a moment before he slams back into me, hard.

I choke as he bruises my throat but it only seems to excite him more. Slowly, he pulls out, only to fall back again and again.

"This feels incredible," he says. "I can't wait to feel *you*." He forces his way down my throat again. "Feel you clench around me." He pulls out just to the tip and though tears run down my cheeks, I'm left wanting.

I suck him harder.

He thrusts back. "Feel you come on me." He pulls out.

The space between my thighs aches. I'm hot all over. Ready. So fucking ready I want to tap just to have my hands finally on his body, to scratch down his back and pull him into me. The memory of his tongue on my clit, the heat of it, the pain in my wrist as he held me down so I couldn't even see him work...

He's out of my mouth and the space he left feels expansive, like I can never be full again. I gasp, ready for more, but already, he's pushed me down, wrapping a strong arm around my waist as his fingertips dig into my waist.

I'm panting. From lack of air, from arousal, from the insane need to have him. All of it. I can't think at all about anything except this.

I love it.

"Please," I beg again as I did the last time we were together.

I need it. I need him.

He stops, the tip of him hovering painfully at my entrance, waiting. I buck my hips up, but he hisses, pulling away from me.

"Please," I say again, this time more urgently. "Don't make

me beg." I can feel my face contort, feel my body move on its own to find him between my legs. It's *painful* without him.

His head dips to my neck, lips running over my throbbing skin. "You tell me to stop, and it stops," he murmurs, then nips at my throat.

I shudder at the sudden sensation. "Yes."

"Say it."

"I say 'stop'," I whimper. "And it stops."

He plants a trail of tender kisses where his teeth just grazed, following the line of my neck down to my nipples as he captures one between his lips and I moan as pleasure radiates through me.

With precision, his hands are around mine again, capturing both in his. He threads his fingers through mine and holds them still as he angles himself against me once again, his other hand pressing on my lower abdomen as his thumb finds the most sensitive part of me. He circles with thumb, and I let out a shuddering scream as he fills me completely.

Soren doesn't wait for me to adjust, or catch my breath. He drives into me, squeezing my wrists until my hands feel numb, and his teeth drag over my shoulder as his hot breath intensifies on my skin.

The intensity of his fingers work in time and he slowly, painfully pulls out and pushes back into me. I don't know how much more of this I can take. Already, I feel the tension in my muscles tighten, a hot coiling in my core intensify. It's one more push into me, the slightest pinch of his thumb and forefinger that sends me tumbling over the edge.

I can feel myself clamp around him, my walls fluttering as he pulls out just a little and I dig my nails into his back. *Don't go.* I scream it, or whimper, or think it. I can't be sure. All I know is the feeling of him drag out of me as I find my release threatens everything.

"I'm not done with you yet," he growls in my ear. His arm loops under one leg and he presses my knee into my chest as he sinks down into me again. The new angle, the strength of him on top of me, the way he's able to effortlessly move and position my body... it's all too much too soon.

But he doesn't stop.

And I don't want him to.

Overhead, the aurora burns brighter.

Something inside me is waking up.

CHAPTER 21

Christmas Magic

The morning comes quickly, and I'm still in awe of how so far north, there's the faintest bit of dawn light. There is magic here, all around me. And within. I can feel the strength in my body, the electric feel of the air. I'm not tired. I'm not stressed. I'm at my best.

Soren and I sit on the library floor, his back resting gently against a tall bookshelf, my body leaning back on his. We're up on the second floor, closer to the sky, and able to see almost the entirety of the space below from here.

It's quiet, and so we whisper, talking about books and stories and the strangeness of our two different worlds.

"You have a magic voice. I could listen to you speak forever," his tone is low, serious about his compliment.

My face reddens at the memory of my cries echoing all through the night.

"And I could listen to you cry out for me every night..." As if reading my mind, Soren pulls me closer to him, one strong arm wraps around my chest, the other across my stomach so I'm flush against his hard frame. His lips graze my neck and shivers race down my back. "I don't want to let you go," he murmurs.

My head falls back to his shoulder, I let him carry the weight of me as I sink completely into his hold.

I know it can't last. Not really.

It never does.

The thought tears my heart in two.

The large door to the library opens, just a crack. For a moment, I worry there will be a parade of elves bursting through, that I'll have to be pulled from Soren's arms and forced to have another horrible breakfast with the princes.

Instead, Vetle slips in, closing the door behind him gently. His eyes scan the room, starting at the bottom level, moving up until they land on us.

I don't know why, but I feel a little guilty as he eyes us. I know, logically, that I don't owe him, or Soren for the matter, anything. And hell, Soren was just turned into a gingerbread as some kind of sick punishment for standing up for us. So he deserves a night of mind bending pleasure.

But that quiet dread melts like a snowflake landing on a hot stove the moment he recognizes us.

Vetle smiles. His usual, bright, excited smile. "You did it!" he shouts and climbs the stairs two at a time in a rush to us.

Soren chuckles, it rumbles along my back as his hands move to massage my shoulders, releasing the tension that gathered there just a moment ago. I look down at my naked form, surrounded by Soren's massive legs cocooning me.

My cheeks burn but Soren's hold is steady. He works out my shoulders still, then his lips run along my neck. "It's okay," he whispers as Vetle crests the stairs.

Vetle, at least, seems completely unphased. He looks at us

like he's walked in on his two friends having coffee. Easy, smiling, content. He bends down to catch my eyes, capturing my chin in his hand gently. "I knew you could," he says quietly. Then, his gaze flicks to Soren. "As a *gingerbread*, though?"

"She broke the spell almost immediately," Soren explains with a light laugh.

Vetle's brows raise. "Thank goodness. I'm a good baker, but I'm not *that* good."

Oh. My. God.

"Excuse me," I hold my hands up, stopping Soren's casual massage. "Wait, I passed the test, so... Where is everyone?"

"Preparing for your debut as Queen," Vetle says with a shrug. "Officially."

I look at the floor, anxiety budding in my chest where affection and warmth had just been. "Does this mean..?" My voice catches in my throat. "That I'll have to choose soon. One of the princes?"

Vetle nods.

I run my hands through my hair, then rest my palms over my eyes. "I *have* to?"

"You have magic. More now than any of us," Vetle says. "The only way to bring Christmas is if you share it with *the* Santa. The king of your choosing." He reaches out for my hands, taking them in both of his. His thumb runs over my fingers gently. "We will still be here. Protecting you."

Soren plants a gentle kiss behind my ear. He nips at it playfully.

Vetle lifts my hands to his lips. "We'll always be here for you," he whispers against my skin.

I sigh, heaviness deep in my core.

I don't want to choose... It was just one night, but being

with Soren has changed me more than the trials ever could. And it's just one morning, but Vetle's easy hold on my hands, the fact that he isn't making me feel guilt or shame for needing both of them...

The magic I feel is perfect here.

There must be another way. I just need to find it.

CHAPTER 22

The Hot Chocolate is Symbolic. Obviously

Dressed in my running gear and Soren in the spare clothes that Vetle brought, we leave the library and with it, any piece of the old me, the one who shrunk and hid, the one who worried and tried too hard while pretending to be detached.

As we leave, I'm more determined than ever to keep this life, my magic, *and* avoid a marriage of convenience. Elisabet said I'd know. That the magic would make me *believe* in my soulmate. But I don't want that either. I don't want to forget them, the affection and hunger I have for them.

We arrive at a door, one with the runes carved in and this time, Vetle turns to me instead of running his hand along it. He quirks a smile and nods to me to approach. "Where to, Annie?" he asks.

I beam at him, then study the door. The strange runes are no longer so strange. I see 'Portal' written into the door. *Well, that's obvious.*

My hand goes up to the wood, and the runes ignite in a

golden glow. "The kitchen," I say, and the order of the symbols changes. It reads 'kitchen'.

I turn the handle, and open the door to exactly where I want to be. Away from everyone else. A place where I can sit and be. Where I can contemplate how to get out of this while also having a good meal.

Leading the way in, with the two close behind, I find my stool at the stainless steel island while Vetle immediately gets to work, pulling ingredients from the cupboards and fridge.

"Soren," he says, his tone uncharacteristically authoritative. "Come here."

Soren raises a brow at me before he does what Vetle asks without complaint.

The two stand beside each other. Vetle is a little taller and leaner, looking at home and confident behind the counter. His easy going expression and happy glances at Soren fill my heart, while Soren, his arms crossing over his body and side eyeing Vetle with an almost playful glare, stokes a fire in my chest.

"I'm teaching you how to make our Queen a proper hot chocolate," Vetle says as he slides a mug to Soren.

Soren looks at the green ceramic as though it will bite him. "I start with heating water?" he guesses.

Vetle nudges him with his shoulder, knocking the frown from his face. "Maybe you can just handle the whipped cream for now."

I watch the two of them work, each nagging the other in their own little ways. It's a dynamic I wish I had seen sooner. I wish I had been able to witness the two of them on their own, without me or the trials, or anything else distracting them.

They're... fun.

My mind turns over escape plans, declarations of independence, telling the princes off. Nothing seems right, and like it or not, I do have a responsibility. One I signed up for, yet still managed to catch me off guard somehow.

I rest my chin in my hand and keep thinking. There's got to be a loophole.

It takes longer than I would have thought to make the hot cocoa. But I also had no idea just *how many* ingredients went into it. I'm used to the instant stuff in powder form. Or, well, I was used to it.

Now, I've come to expect what's in the mug before me: a homemade treat, sweet and rich, a little spice, and a hearty helping of whip cream on top with sprinkles of sugar crystals and a stick of cinnamon to stir. A drink made with heart and joy. A symbol.

I take a sip and my eyes close slowly. I lick the cream from my upper lip.

"See?" Vetle says quietly, as if afraid to break the spell the drink has cast over me. "*That* is why you need to learn."

My eyes flutter open and I catch Soren's grip on the counter tighten as he watches me.

Vetle leans in, his thumb runs along my lips.

Sparks fly through me at his touch.

"Perfect," he says.

I pull back, just a little. "I won't choose one of the princes," I say sternly before I lose my nerve.

Vetle and Soren exchange glances.

"I'll find a way around it." I pull the mug closer to my chest, feeling the heat radiate into my hands gently. "I don't want *that*. I want *this*."

Vetle is the first to look away. His eyes fix to the floor, a crease forming between his brows.

Soren cocks his head. "I don't know of a way to avoid it," he says. "But we won't let you do something you don't want to do. We'll stand by you no matter what."

I sigh. "All I want to do is puzzle this out before I have to see everyone." My eyes dart about the room as my anxiety builds. What would I do about this if I was home? Where would I go? Who would I call to ask for help?

I set the mug down with a hard thud, the whipped cream giggles at the impact. "I want to go for a run," I say as I pull up my first foot to the stool seat. I lace the shoes tighter, double knotting them. When I glance back up, both Soren and Vetle look utterly confused. "I want to go for a run," I repeat quickly. "Alone. I need to think this through." I lace up the other shoe, avoiding their eyes. "I know you're here to protect me and all, but... I have magic now. I don't really know how to use it... but I'm strong. Stronger than I have ever been. I can feel it."

When I finally look up, they both look ready to protest.

"Just a short run," I say, already rising from my seat. "Up the hill and back."

Vetle looks at Soren. He shrugs gently as if to say there's no sense fighting me on this. "Just up the hill," he repeats.

Soren lets out a huff.

"Okay, bye!" I call out before he can say anything else. "I'll be back for the big welcome committee soon! Tell Cat to prep me some red dresses!" I am already at the door before they can speak. "Um..." I run my hand along the door. "Take me to the front of this place. Please."

The runes light up, and I cast one more glance at the two of them before I slip through the door and out into the early morning light.

CHAPTER 23

The Cave is Not a Symbol. Probably

The snow is just cold enough in my lungs to really wake me up. It stings, but in the best way.

I start out slow, making sure my feet are stable on the fresh powder as it crunches gently with each light step.

These shoes are seriously awesome. Or my magic extends to not slipping and sliding embarrassingly on ice. Or some combination of both.

I kick up my pace for an easy jog. I need to move, to tire out even a little, to feel the extra oxygen fill me.

All my best ideas come to me on runs. And it's been too long... Clearly, based on my infatuation for two elves, and my inability to be okay with societal norms outside myself, my brain has rotted from the lack of solo exercise.

The trip up the hill, if I can even call it a traditional hill, is faster than I thought. By the time I'm at the top, overlooking the little village, I'm breathing slightly heavier, but I still haven't come up with a way out of my predicament.

Turning back to the open space ahead, I wonder if I'd be

able to make it to the scattered trees in the distance and back before anyone started to worry.

But just as I am making up my mind, I feel a painful shock in my ears, and the world goes dark.

W hen I come to, there's a horrible ringing in my ears and my head throbs behind my eyes. I roll my head to one side and notice that, while I can certainly move about, there is a strange weight on my wrists.

Cuffs.

Attached to a heavy chain.

I've been locked up.

I pull my hands close to my body and rise up to an uneasy stand as I blink my surroundings into clearer focus.

The space is large with a ceiling so high, I cannot see it. And, it's a little musty smelling. Everything is roughly the same color, with a hint of sheen, a light sparkle in the surrounding firelight that fills the space in an orange and red glow.

The sudden understanding that I'm in a cave hits me just as the giant stalactites and stalagmites come into sharp detail.

What the fuck?

Is this a fourth trial? Like a super secret one?

I move the chain a little, but it's thick and heavy, bolted to the ground with a large stake.

My mind races, thinking of what this could be, a way out. First we had: go get a fire. Then: Ghost of Christmas Present. Next: break the curse of the gingerbread man.

None of them relate to each other in a way that infuriates me.

My eyes move to the shadows, looking for any clues.

There's an undeniable creep factor here. So maybe the trial is one of guts and nerves.

Krampus, maybe?

"Hey," I call out and my voice echoes back at me. "Any tips on what I'm supposed to be doing would be really helpful right about now."

From the darkest shadow, a figure steps forward.

Aksel.

He's in all black, *shocker*, with one hand in his pocket, while the other holds a golden pocket watch. It hangs from his fingers like melting metal. He swings it up in an easy motion, catching it in his open palm as he flashes a wicked smile at me, the one that shows his sharp canine.

If he's trying to scare me, or intimidate me, though, it won't work. I'm fucking pissed.

I grimace back.

"What's this trial supposed to be?" I ask, eyeing the watch in his hands. "Is it timed?"

He laughs, cruelly. "Oh, so you think this is a trial? I thought you were smart, or can you not count to three?"

I roll my eyes, shaking the chain harshly. "The negging isn't sexy."

He pulls back as if I just slapped him. "Sex has nothing to do with it. This is for the future of Christmas."

From the shadows, the other two princes approach. But they keep their distance just like Askel.

Are they... afraid of me?

I look down at the cuffs, there's a coldness at my wrists that I haven't felt since the first trial. Somehow, these chains seem to be holding back my magic.

Even still, the princes are keeping me far from them.

So, it's a proximity thing? I wish I had learned more about how the magic worked earlier. I should have asked more questions when I had the chance. I'm *not* stupid. But I have been distracted.

I harden my stance anyway, my jaw tightens. "If this isn't a trial, then what? Just a good old fashioned kidnapping?"

Aksel lets the pocket watch fall again, it swings gently on its chain, catching the firelight. "You have to pick a prince," he says. "This is just a little... incentive."

Geir steps forward. "These cuffs contain an ancient enchantment welded into the metal. They dull your magic."

I look down at my hand. *No shit.*

He goes on, "An unfortunate thing. Believe us when we say that is the last thing we wish to do."

Isak, feeling emboldened it seems by Geir speaking up, tilts his head. "This isn't a trial, but it *is* timed. You have to choose a king before the aurora lights up the sky."

I glare at him. He's trying to be all poetic but it sounds stupid. "So, night? What time is it now?"

"I would say you have about an hour. Maybe less," Aksel answers.

"And then what? What happens if I just... don't?"

Aksel's smile widens. "Then Vetle and Soren die."

Ice floods through my veins. My heart nearly stops. "You wouldn't." My voice comes out a growl. I'm afraid now, but mostly, I'm *angry*. Angier than I've ever been.

"I wouldn't," Aksel shrugs, casually. "The spell will. Did they not tell you? Too busy using their mouths for... other things."

I let out a shuddering breath. There's no way. No way

they're telling the truth. I search my brain for anything, any clue. Why would there be a time limit on the spell? Why would it hurt the people I care most about? Is it connected to the watch? Can I smash it?

I'd rather fight Krampus.

My eyes rise at last to meet Aksel's. "You're lying."

"Am I?"

I nod. "Yes. You knocked me out to get me here. A place where *they* aren't." I rattle the chains. "You've got me on a stake because you're afraid of what my magic can do. You're trying to force me into a choice I don't want to make because you know nothing else will work. Well, this won't work either."

"Do you even know how your magic works?" Askel taunts.

The chains clink along the ground as I circle closer to them. "I know it's growing. And not because of the trials. But because of *me*. The more I am with them, the stronger I get. I won't have that with you." I look at the others slowly, studying their expressions. They're worried. "With any of you."

Askel sucks his teeth. "We'll see."

"Annie!" Vetle's voice echoes through the cave.

It's like my feet have lifted off the ground with relief. My body tingles with energy. "I'm here!" I cry back as loud as I can. "I'm safe!"

"Foolish human girl," Geir hisses. "You have no idea what will happen–"

"You must pick within the royal line," Isak says, cutting him off. "We have been proven–"

"Annie!" Soren's voice calls.

"I don't need your proof of anything." My voice is firm, unafraid. "I know who I am. I am a Queen."

The heavy sounds of Soren and Vetle's footsteps are behind me. I sense their presence as they draw close, then I feel a crushing embrace as Vetle wraps me up in his strong arms.

"You're safe," he whispers.

Soren stands between us and the princes, his posture ready to fight. "Did you hurt her?" His voice is ferocious. He turns over his shoulder to us. "Undo her chains," he orders Vetle.

I nod, quickly, and Vetle's hands fold over my wrists. The crackle of magic pops around his fingers and the cuffs clatter to the ground as he releases me.

"You have to pick a prince!" Aksel is hysterical now. He leans forward to shout it with everything he has. "You have to pick!"

He reminds me of a toddler in the ice cream aisle, throwing a fit as his tired mother tries to get him to move on. I can't take him seriously.

"I do," I say. I kick the cuffs away from me and the sudden rush of warmth and light fills me again. "I choose *them*."

Soren and Vetle's eyes widen, each turning to me in disbelief.

"You can't–" Askel starts but is silenced when a bright white light shoots through the cave, blinding us all.

When the light finally fades, I find myself not in the dark, dingy cave, but in the middle of the open village, a brilliant northern light shimmering down above us all.

A gathering of elves has formed around me, all excited and smiling. I hear some chant praises, some clap, and others hold each other in joyous embrace. This must be the welcome party.

And here I am in sweaty running clothes and frizzy hair after being held hostage in a cave.

I'd be a little embarrassed, if I wasn't so relieved.

I catch Soren and Vetle's eyes from across the crowd. They look just as confused as I feel. Beside them, the massive fluffy frame of Cat sits peacefully, though her tail thumps into the snow.

"Our Queen!" one elf shouts with joy.

"Where are the princes?" someone asks.

"Who is the new King?" asks another.

"None of the princes will be a king," I say and a few elves nearby raise quizzical eyebrows at me.

I shake my head, and laughter bursts from my throat. I double over, holding my sides. Relief, happiness, gratitude, it all radiates out until I'm glowing. Literally. I'm glowing a golden light. Through my fit of laughter, I rise at last and look down at my hands as they gleam brightly.

I did it. We did it. The magic is strong. Enough to share.

I turn to the closest elf and grab him by the sleeves. "The princes? They're down in a cave. It's massive... and– Do you know it?"

He nods. "There's one not too far from here," he says, confused. "Why?"

"I need everyone there, get the princes and then banish them from here. They'll be serving out a 100 year exile in..." I try to think of the most inconvenient place I can. "In Tucson, Arizona."

The elf raises his brows, but turns to the few others near him and nods to them quickly. "You heard the Queen, let's go."

"They kidnapped me," I call out, a weak explanation, surely. "Yeah, so they deserve it!"

But the elves simply look back, their faces etched with shock. It only lasts a moment before they hurry away.

Well, that was a mood killer.

The crowd's excitement dies down, though a few elves still reach out to me with comfort and kind eyes. "Our Queen," they murmur.

"Our King..?" another elf asks sadly, their head hanging low. "Who will take their place before Christmas now that the princes are gone?"

I smile and hold my hands out until Soren and Vetle approach me slowly. I look up at them, and my glow brightens. Each takes one hand, and I pull them gently to my sides. "My Kings. Our Kings." I hold their hands up and each looks out on the crowd.

Slowly, delicately, they each begin to shimmer. Then, they glow.

It is Cat that disburses the crowd at last, running interference as the elves swarm us. Some to give their congratulations, some to ask eager questions about the legality of it all, and others to express their deep, deep confusion.

Cat moves between the crowd with a quiet ease, nudging people with her head to move along until, at last, it's only us and the quietly falling snow. She looks at the elves, then me and her cheshire cat grin exposes her large, sharp teeth. "I thought this might be the way it would go. Not that I was sure it would actually work," she says. "Sven owes me 100 years of sardines."

"You and Sven need another hobby," I say with a laugh.

Cat tilts her head to one side, a sort of shrug. "I'm proud of you," she says. "I wasn't always sure you had the right stuff. But you did it."

I pull back, but my smile remains. "Thanks..?"

Cat turns to the village, tossing her head over her shoulder. "I'll see to it that the princes are banished. To... Tucson?"

I nod.

"You all better rest up, there's a long season ahead of us." And with that, she disappears into the flurry filled air.

CHAPTER 24
Glow

I am exhausted by the time we make it back to the lodge doors.

I feel like I *should* be celebrating, staying up all night snacking and shaking hands with people, or elves, I'll be spending the next 100 years with. But all I want to do is flop in bed. And maybe take a very long shower.

Alone.

Vetle and Soren follow me as I walk the long way to my room. Neither says anything, and though I feel like since making my choice everything has fallen into place, their silence shocks me.

Still, I was just technically kidnapped (and this time completely against my will) and I just need some time to decompress from it. Perhaps they see that in me. Understand on whatever level that I need time to think about everything, or, not think at all.

We arrive at my door and I turn to them as I touch the knob. "Come in?" I ask, my voice a quiet whisper.

"Of course," Vetle says.

Soren nods.

I look away as my cheeks flush at their stares. "I just..." I open the door. "I need a little time. A long shower."

Vetle smiles. "I'm just glad you're safe. But yes, you do have some dirt on your nose." He ushers me inside. "Take all the time you need."

I chuckle and rub it with the back of my hand. If this were anyone else, any random date, I'd be annoyed. Like everyone else is so perfect, you know? But, right now, I'm glad for him to be real with me. Tell me I got muddied and that it's okay. To take my time. To relax.

I smile back and strip, leaving a trail of clothes all the way to the bathroom.

The shower takes all the time I need. Until I feel finally scrubbed of everything other than my happiness and power.

Time moves differently here, they had said. And it does. I have no idea how long I've been here, under the running water slowly turning my skin red and filling the large space with so much steam it's hard to see. But the best part is that I know I don't need to care.

There's two Kings out there that I *chose.* And they'll wait for me. I know it's no burden on them to take my time.

But, at last, I'm too tired to keep this up and I turn the water off.

I expect it to be cold outside the shower, but it's not. Instead, the warmth radiating off my skin funnels back to me and I feel... So. Damn. Comfy.

I dry myself quickly and, while it's almost completely dark

except for one small torch at the far end of the room, I waste no time climbing into bed where Soren and Vetle already lay, naked and unafraid. There's no discomfort, or awkwardness to them. They both smile at me, each in their own way as I nuzzle between them, naked and dry everywhere except between my thighs.

Still, Vetle covers me quickly under plush blankets, wrapping my body up in his strong arms. I curl into him, pressing one cheek on the side of his chest and tucking my legs between his. The tip of his chin rests on the top of my head and I breathe in deeply.

The scent of cinnamon and spices. It's rich and warm... and hot.

Soren's fingertips trace along my back and heat flares from behind me. I pull closer to Vetle, though my lower back tightens and arches toward Soren.

A sudden need floods into me. I feel so... empty. Heat flares across my face and my stomach at their touch, both tender and teasing. Any ounce of tiredness before is completely gone, filled, instead by an insatiable hunger.

One of Soren's flingers moves between my legs, finding me wet and ready already. He groans as his arm moves to pull my lower back toward him, so close now that I can feel his hard abdomen, his throbbing cock pressing against me.

"Why did you pick us?" Soren asks, his voice so low that I almost miss it between the ringing in my ears.

I gasp as he moves, his cock rubbing along my entrance, threatening to take me at any moment just as Vetle pulls my head up to him, his arms holding my breasts flush against his chest as if to say *answer him.*

And so, with a shaking breath, I say, "It was always going to be you. Both of you. I–"

Soren's tip nudges at me. I can't think straight anymore. He teases me until I buck back, enveloping the head of his cock into me. He gasps at the suddenness of the movement, the ease with which it slid right in. I arch back further, but his large hands cover my hips, steadying me, preventing me from moving.

His moan compels me to try again, and I do, fighting his fingers digging into my skin.

In front, Vetle plants kisses, warm and gentle along my forehead. "Tell us," he whispers. "We want to hear you say it."

I let out a little growl as I fight against Soren's grasp. *I need it. I need him.*

Now.

I clench around the thick tip as hard as I can and his nearly pained groan sends sparks down my back, burning me from the inside out.

He is doing everything in his power to hold back.

It won't be enough.

I wrap an arm around Vetle's neck, my tongue traces his neck and he shivers at the warmth, the feel of my lips against his skin and I am reminded that I have all the power here. They are here by my choice and all the magic that swirls in the room is because of *me.*

"You have a unique kind of magic," I whisper against Vetle's ear. Arching back, I sink down further onto Soren as he sucks in a breath. I turn my head to him, grabbing the back of his neck and pull him down to me so his forehead rests on mine. "Both of you..." I lower myself down his length, feeling his hot breath as he lets out a deep moan. "Deserve..." His hands are steady on my hips, but he lets his grip ease so I can ride back up his length. "To feel…" I feel my body begin to tense, coiling up tight, threatening to explode at any moment. "Free…" I slam back down until he's all the way inside me.

Soren throws back his head, his grip tightens on my hips and I feel the blossoming of bruises where his fingertips hold.

Vetle turns my head back to him, his eyes lock onto mine. "I need you now," he nearly pleads.

I reach down to wrap around him, the massive, hot, throbbing need. I work him up and down, using the beads of precum to ease my movements.

He shudders, jerking up. "Annie," he growls, uncharacteristically letting a primalness take over.

Suddenly, Soren pulls out of me.

The shock of it leaves me gasping, aching to be filled again.

It doesn't last long.

"Take him," Soren orders. "I want to watch you unravel around him."

I don't need to be told again.

I push Vetle back and seat myself around his waist, hovering just above him. My thighs ache at the stretch around him, but it feels incredible, a pain and pleasure greater than any runner's high.

I watch his expression, his mouth gasping open as I easily slide onto him until he fills me completely. My body works to press back up, the ache in my legs and in my core intensifies.

"Touch her," Soren's low voice rumbles.

Vetle's hands find my breasts. He cups one in his large hand, the other runs down my side until his fingers find the space where our bodies meet and he thumbs my clit, sending shockwaves of radiating pleasure through every limb.

I cry out, my head falling back.

"Open your eyes," Soren commands. "Eyes on me now."

My eyes flutter open and lock with his in the dim, flickering light. He grabs my chin as my mouth falls open into a moan.

Vetle's thumb rubs me in intensifying pressure, his hips work in time with my movements to deepen every thrust. I'm about to ignite, about to fall apart, and his steady gaze, intense and domineering, only serves to send me over the edge.

The burning in my muscles, the tight coil in my core snaps and Vetle's hands drop to my thighs as I release around him, coming hard.

"You feel incredible." Vetle's voice comes out a groan. "I'm so close—"

"Not yet," Soren says as he positions himself behind me, wrapping me up in his arms as he pulls me off of Vetle in one strong motion.

Again, I'm left aching at the feeling. I want to be surrounded, filled. Feel them some completely until we're all left quivering and breathless.

Soren lifts me and turns my body quickly to him so I'm straddling him as he sits on the bed. One hand tangles in my hair, pulling me to look up at him. The other, palms my ass, running along the curve of it until he finds my other opening. One digit slides in easily, slick with my own need and I gasp. "Can you take both of us?" he asks, it sounds like a command, but his eyes, warm and steady tell me that he's truly asking, that he will be fine with any answer.

But, *fuck*. I've never wanted anything more in my life.

I nod, but I know it won't be enough for him, so I plead, "Yes. *Please*."

Soren smiles, his finger withdraws. His hand grips me,

lifting me until I'm just above him, weightless. He presses me down on him until he's all the way inside me. I shiver at his sharp intake of breath, the feel of him dragging along my inner walls.

I feel Vetle behind me, and my heart quickens even faster as his hands find my backside. He settles between Soren's legs, nudging at my other entrance.

I sense his eagerness, his building need burning within him. He doesn't want to give me time to adjust, and I don't want it.

I want *this*. I want to be completely filled, safe between them.

Vetle presses into me with an ease I didn't think possible, forcing a sigh from deep within me as he holds on to my hips. "You're perfect," he says, though his breath catches as Soren lifts me up, then pushes me back down onto both of them until they bottom out.

Soren's teeth graze my shoulder and my body responds with a tightening around them both. "Tell me how it feels," he murmurs against my skin.

The stretch, the completeness of them both sends me over the edge again.

"I— I love–"

They move inside me.

Together.

I close my eyes as I feel a hand snake down to my throbbing clit, another hand tightening in my hair, a squeeze of my breast, and a hold on my leg...

My mind goes blank as I ride them through my crashing orgasm, heart ripping through my chest and an explosion of stars lights the room.

I'm shaking, walls fluttering, as I feel the heat of both of them hold me tight between them and spill into me.

I gasp at the feeling.

It's perfect. They're perfect. Both made for me.

Falling

I'm not sure what I expected after my failed attempt at a Christmas party but it obviously wasn't *this*. Falling for two elf guards, discovering magic, and being weirdly okay with leaving behind my old life.

It wasn't sitting in a full chef's kitchen on a comfy stool in a fuzzy white robe, a homemade spiked hot chocolate in hand, watching two insanely hot elves cook for me. In my wildest dreams, I couldn't have pictured myself here – blissed out after a long night in each other's arms, a calm smile on my face and a warmth in my chest that radiates out, literally.

Hell, even having just a jolly Christmas wasn't on my bingo card.

I still don't know what I'll tell my sister. But I do know that it'll probably just be something she'll have to experience for herself. She'll probably just assume I joined a freaky cult where people body modify to have pointed ears when I introduce her to Vetle and Soren. I let out a small laugh, then take another sip of cocoa.

Vetle's eyes flick to me.

Sorne raises a brow.

"I'm just trying to decide how to tell my sister that I'm Queen of the North Pole. And... falling for not one but *two* Santas."

"Falling?" Soren cocks his head. "You've fallen."

Vetle chuckles and goes back to chopping herbs. "So confident," he teases under his breath.

I blush.

Soren's right. I have found myself completely obsessed with these two. I have never felt more alive, more myself, than with them at my sides. Each sparks something different within me, each brings out a side of me long hidden away.

Well, I don't want to hide anymore. And, best of all, I know they won't let me....

I can't predict how things with the other elves will evolve from here, what kind of adventures or challenges we'll discover, or what even the next few days leading up to Christmas will look like.

But I know that, no matter what, we'll face it all together.

And so they all lived
happily ever after.

Acknowledgments

Thank you to my beta readers and unhinged writing group for helping me find the plot between the spice.

A thank you to my husband for not reading this but assuring me every step of the way that I *could* write this. And letting me call reading a bunch of books 'research'.

Thank you to all my loved ones who promised me they would never read this book but still supported me through the journey.

And lastly, thank YOU, dear reader. The world is a big, wild place full of magic and infinite possibilities, but I am very glad you and I have found each other through the chaos. I hope you're having an excellent day when you read this and anytime my words or stories pop into your head, that you take it as a sign of good luck and to go out there and unapologetically do the thing.

About the Author

Calliope doesn't take herself too seriously.

And she hopes you don't either.

Eventually, no matter all our choices and love and pain and attempts at immortality, the sun will go out.
And she thinks that's a really beautiful thing.

With this in mind, she tries to do the maximum good for the maximum time she has... While having fun and being true to herself.

And she hopes you do too.